FARNIGAN'S WAKE

Quail Hill Publishing

Eagle, ID 83616

Visit our website at www.quailhillpublishing.net

First Quail Hill Publishing E-book: December 2015

First Quail Hill Print Book: December 2015

FARNIGAN'S WAKE

A BORIS FARNIGAN MYSTERY

MATT JAMES

QUAIL HILL PUBLISHING

For my Family

CHAPTER 1

Nobody makes house calls these days, even the people who are supposed to, like doctors. Believe me, the only doctors who make house calls work for the coroner's office—and their patients get no benefit from the visit. Only if their business has to do with your home do you get professional house calls. You know, the guys who kill bugs, or who tell you what rotten taste you have in decor, or who rob you of everything while you're out. I am also a professional, one who desperately needs business, and I do make house calls. Call me and I'm there—pronto, before you hang up—if I can get my car started.

Me is Boris Farnigan. I'm a private investigator.

Don't laugh. I know the name is a little incongruous. Believe me, it's a cross I've borne for many a year. But biology is biology, and an Irish father and a Russian mother give you Boris Farnigan. Not to worry, though, the problem is easily solved: I tell everybody to call me Bob.

Now you may be wondering why I make house calls. Fair enough. It's a matter of economics: I have no money, few prospects, and a devotion to eating on a regular basis. Unlike the glamour detectives of stage, screen and the pulp novels, I don't get lucrative jobs. My work is mostly nickel and dime stuff, the kind of income that retains my questionable credit rating.

Except for once, when I was sure the job would be quite lucrative.

It all began on a perfectly fine San Francisco day in the early 1980s. My phone rang. Was I available, could I come right away, and was I discreet? Oh, yes, yes, and yes—definitely. Oh, yes. No big deal. In a matter of minutes I was driving off to take on a case that, hindsight being so damn wonderful, I wished had gone to the guy before or after me in the phone book.

This house call was in one of the better neighborhoods of San Francisco, better as in money, old and new. The Sea Cliff area has homes that on clear days command views of ocean, bay and the hills of the North Bay from their hilly perches. In Sea Cliff the lawns are neatly manicured; the trees, flowers and shrubs impeccably groomed; and the homes, mansions may be a better word, stately. Sea Cliff is a place I can drive through, maybe visit on business, but will never live in, barring a miraculously successful marriage to widowed money.

As my car, an aged Chevrolet Impala, wheezed to a halt in front of my destination, I could sense the disapproval of the neighborhood for it. The Impala looks as if it's in search of a wrecking yard for a final resting place.

So, car parked, I made my way to the entrance to an imposing three storied home with its Elizabethan windows amidst ivy. The door was opened by a disapproving manservant, a thin, bloodless type with pursed lips, who let me into the marbled hallway.

"I have an eleven o'clock appointment with Mrs. Brinton," I announced.

"You are Mr. Farnigan," he told me.

"Right."

"You're late. Mrs. Brinton has been waiting."

"Traffic's bad."

He peered past me through the still open door to gaze at the Impala. "I see."

"It"—I waved my thumb backwards over my shoulder in the direction of the car—"doesn't look like much, but I get a lot of use out of it."

"So it seems, Mr. Farnigan," he noted as he closed the door. "I will announce you to Mrs. Brinton."

Jeeves the Jolly Butler disappeared into a room off to the side where I could hear the hint of his conversation with, presumably, Mrs. Brinton. To kill time, I scrutinized the rich wood paneling, the tastefully expensive artwork, and concluded that I could set an even high fee than the address had indicated.

The faithful old retainer reappeared to lead me to Mrs. Brinton's sitting room.

The sitting room was what one would expect. Again, the beautiful oak paneling, the delicate paintings and statuary; the room was furnished with elegant French-style furniture that easily could have been the resting place for the fanny of Louis XIV. Bright sunlight came through the windows and gave the room a glow that spoke of comfort and grace.

"Mr. Farnigan."

"Thank you, Herbert," Mrs. Brinton said from the love seat in the room's center. "You may leave us."

With yet another dubious glance at me, Herbert departed, closing the door behind him.

"Please sit down, Mr. Farnigan."

She indicated the chair in front of the coffee table, facing her directly. I eased myself into it.

"You'll have coffee?"

"Please." I added, "Black is fine."

As she poured coffee for us from the silver service into the delicate China cups, I studied her. She was, perhaps, fifty and

impressive. What had been a stunning figure in her youth had
become an attractive Junoesque. Even seated, one could recognize that her bearing was tall and dignified. Only a few age lines
detracted from her smooth face and its classical Grecian beauty.
And the large gray eyes, believe me, were unforgettable in their
mixture of authority and sadness. There was a sense of tragedy
and loss in her eyes, in the darkness beneath them, that showed
through her make-up.

"I really don't know how to begin, Mr. Farnigan," she said as
she handed me the coffee cup.

"Begin by calling me Bob—everyone does."

"I thought your Christian name was Boris."

"It is. But that name doesn't go with me."

"I know what you mean," she said with a wan smile. "My
Christian name is Estelle, and I have never felt right about it. It's
a bit much for the daughter of an almond grower from the
Valley. Something simpler, like Jane or Molly, would have been
more apposite."

"I'm afraid I don't see you as a Jane or Molly, Mrs. Brinton."

"Maybe so," she sighed. "It's just I feel nothing like the star-
riness of Estelle these days."

I leaned forward.

"What is your problem, Mrs. Brinton? Why do you think
you need me?"

"A child, Mr. Farnigan. A child who has become an adult
too soon." She paused. "Or, if not too soon—she is eighteen—she
has become a lost adult."

"Her name?"

"Melissa."

"She lives at home?"

"I don't know where she lives."

"I understand."

"You probably do," she said fiercely. "You probably know

about all the horrors children inflict on their parents. I'm sure you've seen all the filth and squalor and hideousness they sink themselves into, killing themselves and their parents."

I should have guessed. A child was always behind one of my visits to a posh neighborhood. A runaway, a kid strung out on drugs with a vicious, blackmailing dealer, or, too often, something worse. It was not the first time I had witnessed a parent's hurt, sorrow, and rage. Those emotions were difficult enough, but the one that truly destroyed the distraught parents of a little girl or little boy lost was guilt. Mrs. Brinton, Estelle, who now wanted to be a simple Jane or Molly, could most likely write a chapter in the book of guilt.

"Of course. It's got to be my fault. My husband Raymond and I failed to do all the things we should have. Money, clothing, cars and the best schools don't substitute for love and guidance, do they?" She glanced at me before answering herself. "No, a good child and a good adult cannot be bought."

"I'm sorry, Mrs. Brinton."

"Thank you, Mr. Farnigan. I'm sure it's an old story for you."

"I'm afraid it is. The worse part of it, as far as I'm concerned, is what I've just heard now—the way parents tear themselves apart. Youth is a terrible thing, Mrs. Brinton, and I'm not sure you can save any child from it."

She asked: "Do you believe that?"

"My experience has been that kids do what they will do despite their parents and themselves. You have to wait and hope and help if you can—if you're allowed to help."

"And it all works itself out," she said bitterly.

"If you're lucky."

"I'm going to try buying some luck, Mr. Farnigan." That made me sit up straighter. The last thing I wanted was to be seen as anyone's lucky chance.

By the time most people call me, the situation is beyond

luck and becomes a matter of clutching at hope. Any hope. That's especially true when errant children are involved. It's only human, I guess, but parents inevitably wait too long, hope too much, before seeking assistance that counts. By counts, I don't mean psychiatrists and social worker types who feed the parents' guilt and tell the kid that he or she is just fine—those people are part of the problem. It's always too late in the game when people like me are called in to attempt to save anything. That's why I hate kid cases—they kill something inside of all the parties involved.

So here we sat, Mrs. Brinton and I, each of us with our own thoughts in a tense quiet.

"You haven't told me what your daughter is doing, what has happened to her."

"It's so difficult, Mr. Farnigan—Bob."

"You have to tell me—or someone else—one of these days."

"Wait here." She arose. "I want to show you some pictures of Melissa."

I stood.

"I have to get them from my room." She headed to the door. "I'll be right back. Make yourself comfortable."

Mrs. Brinton closed the door behind her and I sat back down. Part of me wished that I had not come. She had gotten my name from Charlotte Casey, a mother whose problems with her son had become mine a few years back. Mrs. Casey had been lucky—it happens—and I feared Mrs. Brinton would be overly optimistic because of it. Already, I was short on hope. Why? Because Mrs. Brinton, Estelle, was doing all she could to avoid telling me about Melissa—a very bad sign.

I waited a long time for Estelle Brinton to return, and when she came back into the room her red-rimmed eyes told the story of her delay. It was not the first time I had looked at tear-stained photographs of children.

"This is Melissa," she said as she handed me the photos. The pictures showed a tall, willowy girl with long, straw-blonde hair, a lightly freckled face that reflected her mother's elegant beauty. Whether dressed in a chic gown or in jeans and a shirt, she communicated a disturbing sexuality and an aura of rebellion. In the pictures one could see a promise of misery for all who cared for Melissa.

"These fairly recent—within the last year or so?"

Estelle nodded.

"She's a beautiful young woman."

"She always was. Maybe that was her problem."

"Problem as in men?"

"From the time she was a little girl, she knew that her good looks could get her anything." She laughed without sincerity. "Melissa could do no wrong—her father, my father, any man would tell you that—and believe it. Have you ever seen a seductive three-year-old? Melissa was that, and she knew it." Again, she laughed. "And she held all those men in contempt."

She fussed with the photographs for a few moments before she continued.

"I think she hates men because she can seduce them at will. The only men Melissa has ever liked—if you can call it that—are ones who treated her like trash, like the little slut she became."

I felt uneasy and embarrassed, hating having to listen to Estelle Brinton's pain. For not the first time, I wished I had a different line of work, and I definitely wished I hadn't quit smoking.

"I'm making you uncomfortable. I'm sorry. It's a sordid story."

"That's all right. Don't concern yourself with me." I looked closely at her. "You need to tell somebody. You can't hold all of this inside yourself."

"You know, I haven't been able to talk about this, not really.

Melissa's father—my husband, Raymond—isn't strong enough. Raymond either cries or rages, but he does nothing. Now that she's gone, I think he's relieved."

"Don't be too hard on him, Mrs. Brinton. Reality is hard for all of us to take."

"How true," she said in an abstracted tone of voice. "Raymond's only strong on reality if no emotion is involved." She paused, shook her head, and then continued.

"I used the word slut, Bob, because that is the most appropriate one. Melissa lost her virginity in the eighth grade. Any boy or man who wanted her got his way. It seemed to amuse her. Melissa has had at least three abortions we know of, and I'm sure that she doesn't know how many venereal infections she's had. It means nothing to her."

"I don't see how I can help you..." I began, but Estelle Brinton waved me silent.

"The quality of Melissa's men kept getting worse, especially if they could not be controlled by her seductiveness. One of her 'boyfriends' beat her so badly she had to be hospitalized, and when she was released she went chasing after him for more."

By then, Mrs. Brinton was crying, tears running down her cheeks, but her voice never wavered. There was an iron, untouchable center in that lady.

"Now she has found the ultimate degradation, and she's proud of it. She stood in this very room and bragged to me about her pimp."

"When was this?"

"About three months ago."

I raised my eyebrows.

"I know. But I thought that being a common prostitute would be too much, even for Melissa. I thought she would come back."

"You haven't heard from her since—uh—March or thereabouts?"

She nodded.

"And you don't know where she is."

"San Jose, I think. She said something about San Jose."

"That's a start. I mean, I suppose you want me to find her."

"Oh, yes."

"And bring her home?"

"Only if she wants to come. If she isn't ready, she would leave and only hate me all the more."

"You only want to know where she is and if she's okay. Okay, under the circumstances," I asked.

Again, she nodded. The tears had ceased.

"Did she say what her"—I coughed—"pimp's name is?"

"Randy. That's all—just Randy."

"That's enough of a lead. Surnames aren't that common in that world."

"I suppose not."

"Did she give you any hints of where in San Jose she was, what Randy looked like? Anything?"

"No, nothing at all. She didn't have to be very specific to hurt me."

There was really very little more to say. We agreed on retainer, fee and expenses; she wrote me an advance check; and I left with a picture of Melissa and a dull ache in my soul.

CHAPTER 2

I drove back downtown to my office on automatic, scarcely paying attention to the idiot antics of San Francisco's harried drivers. After my morning, gridlock and its frustrations were almost a relief. If human beings weren't able to figure out how to move cars from one place to another in an orderly way, how could one expect those same humans to have nice, uncomplicated lives? It was enough to drive a man to strong drink, as they say, and which I did when I got to the office.

My office was in an elderly building on Market Street that needed much more vigorous maintenance than it received. It was strictly a walk-in arrangement; you open the door and you're in all the office there is. My receptionist was my telephone answering gadget; the secretarial work was done by my two index fingers and a venerable desk-top computer. The walls were adorned with an old calendar and a painting of the five-and-dime store school of art. My desk, a file cabinet, a swivel chair for me, and two straight-backed wooden chairs for guests were the office's complete furnishings. Believe me, I would rather have had a suite of offices, with delicious looking female help, and all the amenities of prosperity, but times have been tough.

Before the divorce laws got liberalized, I photographed more people in bed than your hardest working pornographer; now most divorce work is limited to jobs for the extremely vindictive, the ones who want to indulge in a little spousal blackmail or voyeurism. Take, for example, the memorable Mrs. Wharton.

"Did you get the pictures?" she had asked.

"Here," I said as I handed her the pictures of her husband with his much younger bedmate.

"Oh, this is good," she leered. "Doesn't he look surprised!"

He did, too; but also, he'd been quick-witted enough to damn near take my ear off with a thrown ashtray.

"I'll show these to my lawyer."

"Who's your lawyer?"

"Richard Allen Clyster—you know him?"

"Heard of him."

"I imagine so. He was the person who recommended you."

"I'd forgotten."

She glared. "You never asked."

"By the way, Mrs. Wharton, why do you need those pictures? You don't have to prove adultery anymore. Divorce is carte blanche."

"Make the bastard squirm, Mr. Farnigan," she said. "Squirm and pay. His dear old mother wouldn't like these pictures."

The wrinkled old bitch made me squirm. I couldn't stand her bony thin-lipped face; she was a wizened creature, worn from her own distillation of malice.

"Speaking of pay ..."

"I know, I know," she interrupted. "You'll be paid when George settles with me."

I guess old George didn't settle. I tried to collect, but Mrs. Wharton had moved, no forwarding address, and I couldn't trace her. Old George might have provided a lead, I suppose, but I doubted if he would have been sympathetic.

My file cabinet was a low, two-drawer type that contained few files. Its chief purpose was as a stand for a Mr. Coffee machine, coffee makings, cups, and a bottle of Scotch. Now that I was back in the office, I sat in my chair drinking Scotch from one of those coffee cups. I have been known to have troubles with alcohol, so I try not to drink too much or too often; but listening to the story of Melissa Brinton's life provided an adequate enough excuse for an early afternoon drink or two. That day I would not be tempted to any self-pity about being middle-aged, unmarried and childless. Well ... maybe about being middle-aged. Believe me, there's no joy in an overweight mid-life, particularly when earning the next meal is getting harder and harder.

I decided to drive to San Jose that evening after dark, when the lower night life begins. It wasn't hard to prowl the streets like a customer, and I might be lucky enough to spot Melissa in a doorway. Failing that, it took no brains to find the bars where the pimps and some of the girls hung out, both professionally and socially. I had confidence in my ability to get a lead on Melissa and/or Randy. Preferably, I wouldn't have to deal with Randy—pimps could get touchy about guys who show any interest in their girls other than the obvious. Believe me.

I looked at my watch. I had three or four hours before the earliest time to begin the fifty-mile drive to San Jose, more than enough time to deposit Mrs. Brinton's check, get some cash, and have a good meal. The Scotch on an empty stomach reminded me of the need to eat. I put the bottle back in the file cabinet, locked up the office, and left.

In the hallway I met Art Burdick, a skinny little janitor I liked, who knew half the people on the wrong side of the tracks.

"What's doing, Farnigan?"

"Nothing much. I might be fighting you for the mop and pail job soon."

He shook his head. "Still no work... that ain't good."

"Actually, I got a client today. Pretty good bucks in it, I think."

Art stood his mop against the wall. He was interested. "So, what sort of case you got, Farnigan?"

"Runaway. You know the story. A kid from a nice family, had all the goodies, but wants to be bad. This kid's gone off to be a hooker."

"An' you're supposed to bring her home?"

"Only if she wants to come. Her mother mainly wants to know if the kid's all right."

"Be careful," he warned.

"Oh, sure."

"I mean it. You know this town's getting rougher, Farnigan. Harry Salomon don't like anybody nosing around his turf."

"Yeah, so I've heard. Harry Salomon's turned into the big man in vice."

"Getting bigger and meaner. Into a lot of stuff, especially drugs."

"Yeah."

"Just so you don't forget who you're up against."

"I'm safe. This kid is working in San Jose."

Art waggled his finger at me. "Salomon has a long reach."

"It's no big deal, Art. I'm sure Salomon's never even heard of this little Sea Cliff runaway."

"Probably. But you back off if he has. You've been around, Farnigan. Salomon likes to hurt and kill."

Art lit a cigar, puffed on it, and spat in the pail.

"Hookers and pimps are bad news, Farnigan. Shit, I was a pimp once—damn mean one, too. Know why I'm not a pimp anymore?"

"You like mopping floors," I suggested.

"Go to hell."

"Come on, Art. Tell me."

"Guys like Salomon, that's why." He spat again. "They move in with money and muscle, and you got to work for them. It ain't worth it."

"You should know."

"Goddamn right. Stay away from hookers unless you're a customer. You'll live longer."

"I'll be careful, Art."

"Sure," he said as he grabbed his mop.

I went on my errands, uneasy because of Art's reminders of what I already knew.

CHAPTER 3

Driving to San Jose on Highway 101 is never a joy, even if you're doing so outside of commute hours. Traffic is always heavy, lanes are inexplicably closed, and every driver near you attempts some kind of bizarre, mad maneuver. That night was no different, and as I passed the Candlestick Park turn-off, I remembered how I used to head out there to watch baseball. I also took in a couple of football games, but baseball was my passion. Baseball creates its own unique world. Believe me, a baseball game is a wonderful universe that moves at its own time, ruled by balance and symmetry in which exceptionally talented individuals have to function at their best, both as themselves and as part of a whole. It is a game of traditions, conventions and subtle mysteries that teaches lessons in patience, honor, pride and achievement. I was a so-so second baseman, but I still dream the summer dream of baseball.

And, of course, like everybody else, I had other dreams and ambitions. I had a good education, including four years at a Jesuit college where I studied English literature and theology, but it does me no good now. I've never quoted Gerard Manley Hopkins or Aquinas to a junkie or a hooker. Maybe I should.

While they were laughing or befuddled I could do all kinds of mischief.

So, despite a good education and a brief stint as a teacher at a boys' school, I drifted into my current profession. A friend, Roy Fleingold, needed a partner. My teaching job didn't work out, and I had seen too many classic Bogart films. I accepted. Soon, however, Roy married a rich client (I think it was mutual blackmail) and I was left without a partner or any real income. I still see Roy occasionally when I have the cab fare; Roy lives in a very expensive neighborhood and the sight of my car would have the homeowners' association and Roy in a rage.

My memories faded as freeway reality brought me back to the present journey to San Jose.

San Jose is a Northern California city that is doing its damned best to imitate the worst of Los Angeles. Congested, smoggy, sprawling, and on the edge of the new money tech behemoth known as Silicon Valley, San Jose had become a large flailing monster seemingly overnight as the life of cities go. When people began to notice the transformation, it was too late to drive a wooden stake through the beast's heart, the best that could be done was to try to contain it. Good luck. Growth spawns growth, no matter how much debris is left behind. Despite desperate attempts at renovation, an old part of San Jose had been left behind, probably beyond renewal. In that area, I hoped to find Melissa.

I parked the car near a recent urban redevelopment sort of building. You know the kind, a glass and concrete rectangle surrounded by ill-tended shrubbery, a monument of Twentieth Century Urban Ugly architecture. Such buildings never really improve the tone of their slummy neighborhood. Instead, the neighborhood absorbs them.

Anyhow, I began walking past the older buildings that were still trying to maintain their dignity amidst the blight and renewal. I passed by a restaurant I had frequented years before, an old Italian place with a ceiling fan, tables with checkered cloths, and plates of inexpensive, filling and delicious food. The smell of garlic, oregano and olive oil wafted out into the street, and I wished I had not eaten earlier. These days the restaurant was a last outpost of civilization, for but half a block away the neighborhood became the Zone.

Every city has its Zone. The place where the pornographic bookstores and movie houses are, where the liquor stores have metal bars across the windows, where the bars stink of cheap booze and despair, and where the prostitutes, male, female and undetermined offer their services. Bare light bulbs and naked neon signs dimly illuminate the scene, but the tint is always a sickly red. Foot traffic is deliberate, a passerby looks at you only furtively, and you have to watch for movement from the shadowy recesses of the buildings.

I walked up one side of the street for three blocks and equally down the other. Sullen looks from drunks and smiles without meaning from the hookers marked my route. As I passed by a doorway to a closed laundry for the second or third time, I heard a voice.

"Can't you make up your mind, fat man?"

A young black woman, maybe in her early twenties, had spoken. She wore a typical hooker uniform—white shorts and an orange tank top that showed off her very attractive figure. Her face had fine features ruined by the cynical curve of her lips as she smiled falsely at me.

"I got what you want," she said.

"Maybe so."

"Oh, shit. A choosy one. It don't matter who you rub it in, fat man."

"That's not what I want."

She looked suspicious. "You no cop—I can tell. You must want something weird."

"I don't want sex. I want a little information."

"Go away, man. Maybe you be no cop, but I don't like questions."

"I'll pay you."

"How much?"

"What's the going price for a trick?"

"More than you can afford."

"I'll pay—and more, if I like your answers."

"Come in the doorway here," she said.

I moved closer to her and showed her the picture of Melissa. "You know her?"

She shook her head, but her eyes darted from the picture out into the street in a look of fear.

"You know her," I said. "You know Randy, too."

"Who's Randy?"

"He runs her."

She made up her mind when I pulled a twenty-dollar bill from my pocket. "She be bad news."

"Why is she bad news?" I asked as I handed her the twenty dollar bill.

"That only twenty."

"You'll get it all. Maybe more. First, you tell me why she's bad news."

"Melissa one crazy white girl. She don't give a damn 'bout nothing. She do anything for money or not. When she do it free Randy kicks shit out of her. But he don't mark her up too much —she good money when she pretty because she do anything."

I handed her another twenty bucks and asked, "So where is she?"

"She gone. So is Randy."

"Where?"

"City." She looked around, again showing fear. "Big man take an interest in her."

"Harry Salomon," I guessed.

"Never heard of him, fat man. People who do, die."

"So I've heard."

A sudden look of dread now filled her face. I could sense the tension of her body as she whispered. "Oh, shit. Here come my man, Dwayne."

I turned from her to see one of the world's larger human beings hurrying toward us. Dwayne was dressed in expensive designer jeans and a mostly unbuttoned steel blue shirt that showed off his burly chest and half a dozen gold chains. I wished I had brought my gun as he stood in front of us.

"What the fuck you doing, Valrina?"

I started to speak but Dwayne gave me a look that killed all speech. He only wanted to hear from Valrina.

"Talk, woman!"

"He just an old weird. He give me twenty if I let him talk dirty. Here." She handed him a twenty. I wondered where the other bill was hidden.

"That all?"

"That's right, Dwayne. He don't even touch me." Dwayne looked at me with contempt.

"All talk. Man, you're sick," he said. "Get the hell out of here."

I went.

In the best of worlds, I would have played the knight errant. In that world, Dwayne would have been beaten to a pulp, Valrina's twenty dollars restored, and my pride left intact. But, believe me, you have to choose your battles and you don't fight on other people's turf where all the advantages—and the muscle —were stacked against you.

All in all, it had been a profitable evening. I was on the trail of Melissa (and Randy). I had gained some insight into Melissa's character (one sick kid) and I had managed to do all this without getting myself damaged (except for a bruised ego). As I drove back to San Francisco one very negative thought oppressed me: did I want to be in pursuit of anyone Harry Salomon had taken an interest in?

CHAPTER 4

S leeping late, not bothering to set the alarm clock, is a luxury that can be indulged in by the idle rich or the marginally employed. Since I was one of the latter, I slept in the next day, waking refreshed and feeling entirely justified because of my evening's labors. Anyhow, I had another, rougher place to visit that night, and I would need to be rested and alert.

I've always been a ten-dollar millionaire. Put a few bucks in my pocket and I become a bona fide free-spender, what they used to call a "high roller." Mrs. Brinton's generous retainer was rapidly depleted that afternoon on indulgences rather than necessities. Books, Bernstein's recording of Missa Solemnis, and good liquor were purchased in hopes of making life a little more bearable.

I really shouldn't have bought the Scotch, however. Over-indulgence in liquor has been one of my many downfalls. Drink, in fact, was what cost me my one and only stint as a school teacher. The administration—it was a boys' school—frowned on a hung over English teacher who told the kids to buy copies of Oedipus Rex as Mother's Day presents. Freud and Johnnie Walker lost me a job.

Let me tell you a story about a sodden afternoon.

I was already drunk and it was only a little after noontime. I was supposed to be teaching the little brats English, but that morning I had phoned in sick. Fear of a fatal hangover had forced me to skip teaching for the cure to be had a Floyd's bar. Floyd's was a depressing saloon. Dark and smoky, smelling of nervous sweat and spilled drinks, the bar was a mournful retreat for the lost. Floyd himself was ageless and hawk-faced, with slicked-back hair and red, sad eyes. He chewed cigars constantly, like Art the janitor, spitting nonchalantly into the buckets that were strategically placed behind the bar.

"You're too young to be drinkin' so early," Floyd said.

"You may have a point."

"I've seen a lot, you know."

"Sure you have." I got off the bar stool. "Time to go."

Out I went into the too-bright sun. Squinting and tearing, I headed toward the bus stop. Suddenly, I was overwhelmed with a desire for scallops. God as my witness, those nasty little shellfish had become an instant obsession. For the moment, my desire for scallops was greater than my lust for drink. I turned the corner in the direction of the local fish market.

I shall not belabor this remembrance of drunks past, but it tells the tale. I reached the fish market and discovered no scallops - they were out of season. Belligerence set in and I accused the fishmonger of hoarding scallops for his own unnatural sexual practices. Great hands smelling of fish and smeared with fish guts clamped onto me and threw me out of the market.

There's a lesson in this story, but I'm not sure what. Sure, I control my drinking a bit these days; but that is probably a matter of getting older, not anything like reform. Believe me, I don't know why I drink or don't drink.

In late afternoon I finally showed up at my office and began to feel some guilt over my earlier extravagances as I surveyed the bills, due and past-due, the mailman had delivered that morning. The bills were deposited in the bottom desk drawer with their predecessors and then I hit playback on the phone answering gizmo. The disembodied voices offered no hope of financial salvation. There were two wrong numbers, a taped sales pitch, and a demand for payment from someone whose bills had gone into the lower drawer too often. Despondency had begun to creep over me when there was a knock on the door. Art the janitor and forcibly retired pimp entered.

"How did your snooping go last night, Farnigan?"

"Fun and games, Art. Sit down and I'll tell all about." Art sat and I talked, with me portraying myself in the best manner at all times.

"Poor girl," Art said when I finished.

"Which one?"

"Actually, either one." Art lit a cigar. "Both of them are in trouble. Your talkety hooker probably had the crap knocked out of her by Dwayne."

"No reason for that."

"Hell, Farnigan. Dwayne, if he's any kind of pimp, knows she held out some of the money you gave. It's part of the game. So he takes it and beats on her. Dwayne ain't much of a pimp if he lets old Valrina get away with holding out on him. And she knows that, too. It's a game, like I say."

"You used to beat your girls?"

"Hell, yes. It was expected." He shook his head. "But I wasn't like some guys, you know, the ones who get their thrills with their fists."

"You're all heart, Art."

"Damn right," he agreed, ignoring the sarcasm.

I offered drinks from the bottle on the file cabinet.

Art looked like a resident of the garden of earthly delights as he relaxed with Scotch and a cigar. And he was in a mood to talk. "Melissa is in trouble, too, now."

"What do you mean?"

"Harry Salomon. He's always trouble for two kinds of people. People he takes an interest in; and people who take an interest in him."

"Not me. I only want to talk with Melissa."

"So what?"

"It's not that I'm trying to take her away."

"Maybe Harry won't see it that way. If he has taken a personal interest in her…"

"You mean a really personal interest, don't you?"

Art nodded.

"I thought Salomon had merely brought her up to the City for business reasons, you know, sort of a promotion."

Art laughed. "Harry Salomon lets the little men handle that sort of thing, Farnigan. Harry's an executive, not a talent scout. If Harry took notice of Melissa, it was for his private purposes."

I said nothing and Art continued.

"Harry is a man of cruel tastes, if you know what I mean."

"A sicko?"

"That's being too kind."

"I didn't know that about Salomon," I admitted.

"You don't know much about him, do you?"

"I guess not. Believe me, I stay clear of guys like him. Hell, I only really saw him once, when someone pointed him out to me."

"Harry's bad news, Farnigan. Give the Brinton woman her money back."

"I can't."

"Spent it?"

I nodded.

"Tough luck."

I poured each of us another drink.

"When you told me that this Melissa kid had the reputation for doing anything, I knew it was bad for you," Art said. "She's just the girl for Harry Salomon."

"So he takes her from the streets of San Jose to be his city girl?"

Art looked disgusted. "Cut the romantic bullshit, Farnigan. Harry Salomon didn't take her in—he uses her. When not with him she's on the streets. Harry wants her to make money for him, he's all business. That's the way Salomon works."

"Poor kid."

"Damn right, Farnigan. Likely as not she ends up dead."

"Why's that?"

"I told you. Harry Salomon has strange ways. Sex and death are all mixed up for him. Harry's girls end up dead."

"Good lord."

"Back off, Farnigan," Art warned. "Harry Salomon is why I'm a janitor. I'm lucky I'm alive." Art stood up. "You don't strike me as a lucky man."

"Thanks."

"Word to the wise."

"Sure."

"And thanks for the drinks."

Art left.

What to do, I thought, was to forget this entire thing.

Art Burdick couldn't have done a better job of scaring me off if he was a muscle man for Harry Salomon. Yet, somehow, I didn't want to leave myself out of Melissa's sad story, even if it meant crossing the path of someone whose very name frightened braver men than me. I don't see the world like some soupy lady novelist, but I suspect Estelle Brinton had a lot to do with my feelings. There was something about a real lady like Estelle Brinton that made me want to set her world right for her. It was her elegance and her vulnerability, her beauty and her grief, and her dignity and her sorrow that had touched me. Perhaps, too, it was the wish of a childless, middle-aged man to save what was left of a family, to save the daughter I would never have. Maybe, too, it was sheer stubbornness—or a death wish. I don't know.

Believe me, it does not pay to examine one's motives in a dark office with a bottle of Scotch. I was more than a little bit rocky on my feet when I finally left the office for dinner. The old line about a condemned man's last meal nagged at me while I ate what was, I think, a good dinner.

CHAPTER 5

"Farnigan!"

I turned and saw Gene Winston.

"Long time," I said as we shook hands.

"Years, I guess," said Gene. "What brings you to the Tenderloin? Business or pleasure?"

"You know I can't afford the pleasure."

"Still broke. It figures. So it's business."

"I'm looking for a girl."

"Runaway?"

"Sort of, I guess. She's legally an adult, but she's run away from a better life than down here."

Down here being the Tenderloin, San Francisco's vice district, a section of the city that trades in every desire of the flesh for a price. Hookers display themselves in the doorways of the seedy hotels; garish neon lights advertise porno bookstores and movie palaces; bars offer the comforts of booze and bare-breasted dancers. For a price, a man can sauna with a bored prostitute, or get a "massage" in one of the parlors, or sit on a cushion in a dark, stuffy room and talk dirty to a naked girl. Pimps patrol the streets in their cars keeping wary eyes on their women; dope dealers make their rounds from place to place, and bored-looking cops cruise by on the look-out only for the sudden violent crimes that happen as the hour grows late.

Gene Winston has tended bar in the Tenderloin for about thirty years. His hard eyes tell all you'll ever know about what he's seen. While we stood on the corner of Turk and Eddy I wondered how guys like Gene and I ended up where we were, how the Jesuits who had gotten both of us through high school would judge our lives as men.

"It's cold out here, Farnigan. The goddamn wind and fog get colder every year I live."

I asked, "You working?"

"On my way."

"It's almost midnight."

"We stay open all night." He laughed. "We get busted once in a while for being open after hours, but nothing comes of it."

"Good honest job, Gene."

He shrugged. "Keeps me fed."

I reached into my coat pocket and took out the picture of Melissa. Gene gave it a glance.

"I've seen her."

"Her pimp's name is Randy."

"I know him. He's a loser. His meal ticket caught a big shot's eye."

"Harry Salomon."

"I didn't say that." Gene looked uncomfortable. "You can ask Randy all about it."

"Where?"

"He drinks full time at the Velvet Devil these days. Know the place?"

"I've seen it."

"It's a tough joint, Farnigan. Bartender is Jack Ford—he's

okay—but forget about the rest. In fact, you're smart if you forget this Melissa bitch."

"I know. But I've got a dumb job and it makes me do dumb things."

"Suit yourself, Farnigan. Just a warning—for old time's sake."

"I appreciate it."

"Sure," he said. "Got to go now. Can't be late."

I promised Gene that I would come for a drink at the bar he tended one of these days, although Gene hadn't given me its name. That's the way it goes.

He started to walk away when I asked, "What does Randy look like? I don't know."

"You're making me talk too much."

"Hell, I'm not asking for a goddamn letter of introduction."

Staccato-like, Gene said, "Thirty, big, stupid, and all pimples."

"Jesus."

"Mean son-of-a-bitch, too. Thinks with his fists. Even his mother probably hates him."

That was that, our conversation was really over. Gene wandered off into the red neon lit fog and I headed off for the Velvet Devil.

Gene Winston was no liar and he hadn't slandered the Velvet Devil. The moment I entered I wished I was back on the street where at least a man has some running room. The place had the strong sour stench of cheap booze, cheaper perfume and stale smoke. The tobacco haze burnt my eyes as I glanced over the dimly lit crowded room. All the stools at the bar were taken, so I joined the standing-room-only folks at the end where I bought a Scotch and water. At the opposite end of the room, a couple of middle-aged men stood at a pool table having an apparent argument. Customers who spoke softly and saw everything filled tables and booths. I was a stranger they were assessing, passing judgment on.

It wasn't hard to spot Randy. Any man who has a table to himself in a crowded bar is obvious. His being alone told all about his character. Believe me, I did not want to be the one to break the ice.

"Buy a girl a drink, Farnigan." The whiskey-toned female voice cut through the low murmuring. I glanced around again and saw a woman waving at me from one of the tables. It was Sally Jackson, a long time (and aged) practitioner of the oldest profession.

I made my way over to her table.

"Looking for me?" she asked in tired seductive voice without conviction.

I shook my head.

"Just as well." Another woman, younger, was at Sally's table. Sally spoke to her.

"You go now, Christine. Nothing's happening here. Carl don't like you girls sittin' around all night. You got work to do."

Christine muttered something and left. I sat down.

"It's a bitter cold night you sent Christine out into," I said.

"She has to pay her dues. You get old like me and you can start telling the other girls what to do."

"You and Carl partners now?"

"Hell, no!" She laughed. "I'm just his oldest hooker. But I look after the others for him."

"I see."

And I did. Sally was only in her early forties but much the worse for wear. Too many late nights, too much drink and drugs, and far too many anonymous sex partners had taken their toll. Her heavy makeup could not hide the wrinkles and sagging weariness of her face, and although she still had a great figure she could not disguise its mature broadening.

"Oh, I still turn my share of tricks, but not like when I was young."

"We all slow down."

She laughed. "Especially you men. Give me a young man anytime. They hardly start before they're done. You old farts have to work at it."

"Thanks, Sally."

"I am the expert."

We laughed. And when she laughed I saw her as she was fifteen years ago, young and beautiful, when she had hired me to help her brother out of a jam. I had done a good job and had never lost track of Sally.

"You working tonight, Farnigan?"

I nodded in Randy's direction. "I'm looking for someone and need to talk to Randy over there."

"You're looking for Melissa."

"Got it first guess."

"Randy's not likely to help you."

"No?"

"He lost her to Harry Salomon." She lit a cigarette. "Randy's angry and scared. He's plenty pissed off at Harry, but Randy knows he's dead if he tries to get Melissa back. So, he sits around drinking. He's a bad one."

"I still have to talk to him."

"Maybe I can help. Randy likes me—God knows why—maybe because I listen to him."

"You could introduce us."

"Sure Farnigan, I will. Just don't come on too strong with him. Randy is drunk and mean. He could take you."

"I believe you."

We stood and made our way to Randy's table. Before he could focus his red-rimmed bloodshot eyes we had seated ourselves. Believe me, ugly was an inadequate word in relation to Randy. Melissa's self-hatred had to be monumental to attach herself to a hulking gargoyle like him.

"Hiya, Sally," he muttered. "Who's your friend."

"Just a guy I know, Randy. He's no trouble."

Randy glowered at me. "You better not be no fuckin' trouble. I've taken enough crap lately. I'm ready to dish some out."

"Don't get steamed at me, Randy. We've got the same bad luck."

"How's that, fat man?" Randy looked suspicious.

"Melissa."

"That bitch!" He exploded. "She's nothing but trouble." He laughed. "But she'll end up dead. All his women do."

I said nothing, so Randy continued.

"She likes his little games, the ultimate weird thrill. Screwin' with him is a matter of life and death."

"I want to see her, Randy."

His eyes narrowed. "Who the hell are you, man?"

"Hold on, Randy. It's okay."

He looked at Sally who nodded. Randy relaxed a bit. "I'm Melissa's uncle," I lied. "Our family is worried about her."

"You should be. She's finished." He shook his head. "I don't care about her, you know. She's crazy. But she earned me good bucks while it lasted. 'Til she goes off with him."

"You're talking about Harry Salomon."

"Maybe," he said slowly, looking back and forth at Sally and me. "Some things it don't pay to talk about."

"That's fine by me," I said. "I just want to see Melissa."

"That's easy."

"It is?" I was surprised.

"Hell, nights she ain't with him she's working. You know what I mean?"

I nodded.

"She don't do the streets anymore. He's getting top dollar for her now." He snickered. "From people with special needs."

"So how do I see her?"

"She lives at the Hopkins Hotel. Don't go there and ask for her unless you want the shit kicked out of you. Got that?"

"I hear you."

"Good. But you can see her when she goes out, you know, when she's going to work—just those nights. It's different, her nights with him."

"She goes on foot?"

"Down to Union Square. She gets a cab there."

"About what time, Randy?"

"Six, maybe seven, in the evening. It changes."

"I bet."

"It's regular enough."

"I believe you, Randy."

"I don't believe you, man. You ain't no uncle." I started to speak but Randy kept talking. "Don't bother me. I don't care who you are. I just hope you mess him up."

"Harry Salomon's none of my business. I only want to see Melissa."

Randy snorted. "Good story. Tell it all you want." There was a long silence. Randy got up and stumbled to the bar.

"He telling me the truth, Sally?"

"I think so, Farnigan. He hopes you'll take Melissa from Salomon. I think Randy would help anybody take her from him." Her voice throbbed with contempt. "Randy's a small time pimp. He's mad because Salomon pushed him around. Randy knows he can't do a goddamn thing, but he'll help any fool who wants to mess with Salomon."

"I'm the fool, I suppose."

"Right on the first guess."

"Touché."

Randy lurched back with another drink. His mood had gotten uglier.

"I drink alone."

Sally and I said nothing as we left Randy to nurse his bitterness. As we walked toward her table she suggested that I keep on going. It might keep me healthy longer.

I took the advice.

CHAPTER 6

The next two nights were a complete waste of time. Believe me, time alters itself into the essence of slowness when you have to stand, helpless, waiting. When you're watching a place you have to be alert. It's not time to catch up on your reading or to work crossword puzzles. Sure, you can play mind games with yourself, solve the world's problems, or even figure out just where your life went wrong. But that's boring stuff, believe me. Oh, yes, I forgot to mention that you also have to do all this standing around without drawing attention to yourself. That's the worst of it. Years ago, I was working on a case where I had to watch an apartment building to keep track of adulterous comings and goings. That job nearly got me killed. On the third or fourth night a guy came running out of the building shouting at me. It seems he thought I was looking at his 1965 Mustang with dishonorable intentions. He wanted to wring my neck. A lot of talk and a hasty retreat had been made. Ever since then, when I have to watch a place I look for a 1965 Mustang right away.

Anyhow, I had spent two nights across the street from the Hopkin's Hotel with no success in spotting Melissa Brinton.

Presumably she was off doing whatever she did with Harry Salomon. Or she had moved. Or, more likely, Randy had lied to me. A coffee shop directly across the street provided me a good place to sit and watch. So for two evenings I had drunk too much coffee from five to eight o'clock. I had little choice. The Hopkins Hotel was the best lead I had, even if my faith in it was weakening. I'm not a patient man, which is a serious liability for a detective, and I had to resist the temptation to give up too soon. Besides, I didn't much care for the thought of having to retrace my steps for a new lead.

I suppose a place like the Hopkins Hotel might still have a few good rooms, but it gave the impression of being just another Tenderloin hotel that specialized in half-hour occupancies. The lobby was bare and dirty, the front desk enclosed like a cage, and a smell of mildew and hopelessness pervaded it. The clientele consisted of hookers and their johns, drunks on welfare, and, sadly, the elderly urban poor. It was a depressing building in a rotted part of the City. Merely looking at it added to the sense of despair I felt.

On the third night Melissa came out of the lobby door.

She was prettier than her photographs had led me to believe. Her clothes were expensive, no doubt to satisfy her select clientele and Harry. If a hooker could look elegant she did —a legacy of Estelle Brinton's gone bad. As she stood on the sidewalk facing me in the coffee shop, I thought again how her beauty was marred by her spoiled, rebellious expression. Melissa turned and began walking in the direction of Union Square. I followed.

She was a fast walker, and I had to move faster than I like to in overweight middle age. I was nearly out of breath when I caught up to her.

I said, "Melissa. I have to talk to you."   .

She stopped, looked at me. "Fuck off."

"Your mother sent me."

"How sweet," she sneered. "Mommy wants her little girl to come home and play house."

"She cares about you."

"Bullshit. She's scared that I'll turn a trick with one of her fancy neighbors. That would shame her."

"That's unfair, Melissa. She wants to know if you're doing all right. Your mother wants to help if you're in any trouble."

"So she sends a fat old man. She's probably not even paying you enough to afford an hour with me."

Disgust and anger choked me. I could barely squawk out my words.

"You're not worthy of her."

"Lady Estelle got you, too," she laughed. "She play the injured great lady for you?"

"Shut up, Melissa."

She turned and began walking. Other people passing were giving me strange looks, no doubt wondering why I was hassling poor Melissa.

"Wait." I rushed after her.

"You're in my way," she said with barely controlled anger as I stood in front of her, blocking her.

"You're going to talk to me."

"There's nothing to say to you. I live as I want to. That means without you or dear Mommy or anyone else."

"You prefer Randy or Harry Salomon."

"Randy's a creep, a nothing."

"Right. Harry is a much better sort."

"Don't talk about Harry. He steps on fat bugs like you."

"Maybe you and Harry deserve each other."

I should have noticed the car that had stopped on the street behind us. It's hard to miss spotting two guys who are so obviously bad news. Anyone could have looked at them and known that they made their living by dismantling other folks. But I missed all that until they stood next to me.

One of them spoke to Melissa. "This guy bothering you?"

"Yes."

A hand gripped my arm. My new friend said, "I have a gun in my pocket."

I looked into his gray eyes and believed him.

"He wants me to be a good little girl," she said. They all laughed.

"He mouthed off about Mr. Salomon."

"That's real dumb," said Gray Eyes. "But we know what to do about that."

His partner, a man with a permanent smile that meant nothing, told me to walk to the car.

"Listen, I wasn't doing any..." I started to say, but Smily told me to shut up.

As we walked to the car I heard Melissa's voice. "Beat the shit out of him."

Gray Eyes drove while Smily kept me company in the back seat after he had frisked me. The gun Smily held pressed to my side discouraged conversation. We drove in silence across town towards the warehouses in the China Basin area. It was growing dark and the streets were empty.

"Fat guy's got a big mouth," Smily said.

"Too bad for him," Gray Eyes replied as he drove. "You think we should close it permanently?"

"No. He's not worth a murder rap."

"Guess so," said Smily.

"But we can hurt him some."

Smily brightened. "Hear that? We're going to teach you how to keep your mouth shut."

I said nothing.

Gray Eyes said, "See, he doesn't like to talk already." The

car pulled off of Third Street. We drove down an alley between closed warehouses.

"This looks good," said Smiley.

Gray Eyes nodded and stopped the car.

"Get out," said Smiley.

We stood between the car and the warehouse. My back was to the wall with the two muscle men facing me.

"What's your name?" asked Gray Eyes.

"Farnigan. Boris Farnigan. People call me Bob," I replied lamely.

"They call him Bob," Gray Eyes told Smiley.

"That's nice."

Without warning Smiley kicked me in the groin. I fell to the ground, dizzy and nauseous, writhing in pain.

Gray Eyes said, "Now you've gone and hurt Bob before I could ask him what he does for a living."

In reply Smiley bent over me and took my wallet from my back pocket. Before walking back to his companion to inspect the wallet Smiley kicked me in the back.

"You hurt him some more."

"I know. I'm just a mean bastard." Smiley was quiet a moment. "Papers here says that Bob is a private investigator. Must be a bad one, he's only got twelve bucks in here."

The pain was beginning to ease as they talked on and on about what a lousy P.I. I was. They were enjoying themselves. I wondered if I had a chance to escape if I could hide from them in the maze of warehouses, discarded empty packing crates and dumpsters. No such luck. They were standing next to me, conversation ended.

"Kick him again," said Gray Eyes.

My shoulder exploded in pain, my arm going immediately numb, when Smiley delivered his expert kick. I curled up in pain.

Gray Eyes said, "Tell us who you're working for."

"Melissa's mother." I gasped. "She just wants to know that the kid's all right."

Another kick from Smiley. This time to the side around the kidney.

"Then why are you talking about Mr. Salomon?" Gray Eyes asked.

"I heard the name."

"Where?"

"Around. I don't remember. I talk to a lot of people." Another kick to the same shoulder. I groaned. "You should mind your own business, Farnigan." I couldn't tell who said that, pain distorted my perception.

Smiley said, "This will help teach you to mind your own business."

I was dragged to my feet. They took turns, one holding me while the other quickly and efficiently worked me over with his fists. During Smiley's second turn I blacked out.

I came to at about three in the morning. The taste of blood was in my mouth, my left eye had closed, and every nerve in my body shrieked with pain. I stumbled to my feet, found my wallet on the ground with my money still in it, and began staggering down the alley toward Third Street.

A couple of cabs on Third Street passed me by before one finally would stop for me. Believe me, when I saw how I looked in the rear-view mirror of the cab, I didn't blame the other cabbies for not stopping. The cabbie agreed that the emergency room of San Francisco General Hospital was a good choice for a destination.

There were no real questions raised at the hospital—they see a lot of guys who have lost fights. A young doctor was, I think, amazed when he told me that I had no major damage. A concussion, three cracked ribs, a slight shoulder dislocation and a couple loose teeth were the worst of it. The doctor put stitches in above my left eye. He wanted to keep me for observation, so I had to sign a paper saying that I understood that I was leaving against medical advice. Everybody has to protect themselves against lawyers.

CHAPTER 7

My recuperation was uneventful. Damned boring, in fact. I confined myself to bed for two days, leaving only to care for pressing bodily functions. No one has ever eaten as much canned soup as I did those several days, supplemented by a couple bags of potato chips. The salt on the potato chips provided a vivid, painful reminder of the effect fists have on a mouth.

It probably should have hurt my feelings that absolutely no one telephoned while I was laid up. Even my creditors were curiously silent. They missed a great chance to kick a man when he was down. The few people who care about me—Fred, Elizabeth, Father Dan—aren't given to phoning too much or too often. I'm usually out anyway. Yet, they hear from me pretty regularly, so it was, I guess, a little odd that no one missed me. I really didn't think that I needed any more humbling, but one's opinion in such matters apparently does not count.

The worst of it all was my inability to get comfortable. I hurt in too many places for that. Yet I did get a lot of rest and I began to feel better. I knew I was on the mend when I could concentrate enough to read.

On the third day after the encounter with Melissa and her friends—it was a Tuesday—I faced up to having to contact Estelle Brinton. Believe me, the beating had been bad enough, but having to talk with Mrs. Brinton made my soul ache. It was about three o'clock in the afternoon when I walked into the living room, still in my pajamas, to dial Mrs. Brinton's telephone number.

"The Brinton residence," announced the snotty, disembodied voice of the butler, Herbert.

"This is Mr. Farnigan. May I speak to Mrs. Brinton?"

"One moment."

There was a long silence before Estelle Brinton's voice came over the line. My throat tightened when I heard her hopeful tone.

"Mr. Farnigan—Bob. It's so good to hear from you."

"Thank you, Mrs. Brinton."

"You have news for me?"

"Yes. I found Melissa."

"Where?"

"In the city. Where you'd expect—the Tenderloin."

"I see," she said. After a pause she asked, "Melissa is all right, isn't she?"

"Not really, Mrs. Brinton. Your daughter is involved with some very rough, very bad people."

Estelle Brinton said very softly, slowly and not as a question, "Then I've lost my little girl."

"I'm afraid so."

"You did talk to her?"

"I tried. But she's beyond listening to anyone, I think."

"I'm sure you tried. We've all tried."

"Mrs. Brinton, Melissa will come back only if she wants to. There's no way to make her come back, and these are people who would stop that anyhow."

"I don't understand."

"There are men watching over her. She's a valuable commodity—I can't think of a better, nicer way to say it—and anybody who interferes will be hurt."

"Were you, Bob?"

"Yes, I was. Some of her protectors roughed me up pretty good a couple nights ago."

"How awful!"

"I'll live. They knocked me around—did a good job, too—but I'll be back in shape in a few more days."

She said, "I have to see Melissa."

"You don't want to go where she is."

"I don't care about that. I have to talk to her. She's my only child."

"Mrs. Brinton, there's no way you can speak with her where I found her. It's too dangerous—for both of you."

"You're frightening me, Mr. Farnigan," she said reverting to formality.

"I mean to. You have to understand that Melissa can't be approached now—at least not in the open."

I could sense Estelle Brinton struggling to retain control over herself during the long silence that ensured. "You could arrange it," she said at last.

"Arrange what?" I asked with the sick feeling that I knew the answer.

"You could see Melissa, Mr. Farnigan—I mean, Bob—and find a way for us, Melissa and I, to meet."

"I don't think you understand."

"I know it's dangerous," she interrupted. "And I wouldn't ask you to do it if I could think of another way. I'm desperate."

It was my turn to be quiet. A less than noble side of me advised me to end the conversation, forget Estelle Brinton and Melissa, and look for another line of work. My better self (or more foolish self, if you're a cynic) urged me to agree to make one more contact with Melissa, risk and all, because I did want to help Estelle Brinton If I could. And, yes, there was an element of pride, call it professionalism, that didn't want to admit that I'd been scared off of the case.

"Are you still there, Bob?" My ruminations were ended abruptly by Estelle Brinton's question.

"I'm thinking all this over."

"I know I'm asking a lot."

"It can be done, even if I'm a damn fool for doing it."

"Thank you, thank you so very much." There was relief in her voice. "Any chance means so much to me."

I cautioned, "It may come to nothing. Melissa isn't much on listening to anybody."

"But we have to try."

"Yes, we do." I sighed.

She thanked me some more; her gratitude was almost painful.

"I'm going back to the Tenderloin tonight," I said. "If I have any luck I'll see Melissa and ask her to meet with you. It will be up to her to name time and place if she does agree."

"I understand. I'll be available for anything."

And she would be. That was the way of a lady like Estelle Brinton. We spoke a bit more, mainly an attempt on my part to keep her from being too hopeful. Before I hung up I promised to inform her immediately of anything—for good or bad.

I proceeded to shower and then to shave. My face as reflected in the bathroom mirror would have been a good one to threaten naughty little children with. The stitches above the left eye were ugly, the scrapes and bruises on my face were purple and puffy. The portrait of a literally beaten man, I thought bitterly. Still, I took a little consolation from the fact that I had a mostly full head of hair and that my long, sad-eyed face was not too ravaged by age. Believe me, you take what you can get at times like that.

Dressing was no joy, my whole body was still stiff and sore, especially my shoulder. It took much longer than usual to assemble myself in my accustomed sartorial splendor. By the time I was finally ready to leave I was hot, sweaty and weak. My hand shook as I put my .38 revolver in my right coat pocket. It was nearly five o'clock. I decided to leave my car home again and took a taxi to the Tenderloin.

CHAPTER 8

The coffee shop across from the Hopkins Hotel was as dismal as always, the coffee as oily and weak-bitter. The counterman recognized me and observed that I looked like hell. Since I was feeling bad already, I decided I couldn't hurt myself anymore if I ordered some food from him. A plate full of greasy fried chicken and lumpy mashed potatoes appeared. After all the soup and potato chips, the meal was a feast. I even said something nice about my dinner when I paid for it. The counterman looked at me with amusement. The way my stomach was already beginning to feel I couldn't blame him.

Melissa almost caught me by surprise when she emerged from the hotel. It was only a little after six, early for her, I thought. She was dressed in a variation of the high price tart look, a tightly fitting dress with a slit all the way up the side to her upper thigh. Melissa wore dark glasses and carried a small drawstring purse. As before, after pausing for a moment, she began walking briskly in the direction of Union Square.

I rushed out of the coffee shop, aching with the effort, in pursuit. There were more people on the street that evening, and nasty looks and words assaulted me as I half-ran, half-trotted after Melissa. A terrible sense of déjà vu and of impending disaster flooded over me as I caught up to Melissa at almost the exact spot as three days before.

I panted, "Melissa! Stop! I have to talk to you."

She turned quickly, facing me directly. Her mouth was twisted with hatred and contempt.

"Get out of here, you bastard," she hissed.

"I want no trouble."

"You're trouble," she said. Her hand grabbed her sunglasses, lifting them briefly. One eye was blackened. "Get out, go away!"

"Melissa, your mother wants to see you. Any time, any place —your choice."

"Goddamn her!"

I reached toward her. She backed away.

"Don't touch me. Stop bothering me."

"I mean you no harm."

"You all do. All the nice people. They even hire assholes like you to hassle me."

"You've got it wrong, Melissa."

Tears were streaming down her cheeks from behind the sunglasses. Her voice was high and shrill with emotion. "I don't want my mother or her world. Why won't any of you under-stand that and leave me alone!"

"We're only trying to help you."

"Help," she snarled. "You're going to get me killed."

"You're wising up, Melissa."

"Fuck you, old man. I'm not in any trouble as long as you people leave me alone."

"The people who love you."

"Love is a fool's word for a piece of ass. We all get paid one way or another for it. My mother spreads her legs and gets to play rich lady. God knows what you get."

"Melissa, at least talk to her. I'll keep coming back 'til you do."

"No, you won't. Don't you remember how your face got messed up?"

I patted my coat pocket. "I brought a friend this time."

"You stubborn bastard! I hate you. I hate all of you. Can't you leave me alone!"

"No, Melissa."

"I can't take this. You're messing up everything. I won't have you chasing me."

"I have to."

"Please go away from me. Tell her I'm gone. Tell her I'm dead."

"Tell her yourself."

"I'll never talk to her."

"You will," I said. "You will because I'll find a way to make you."

"You mean that," she said in a cold, detached voice. "As usual, what I want makes no difference."

I nodded.

Melissa took three or four steps backwards from me. Her hands were fumbling as she began opening her drawstring purse. "I wish you were my mother standing there," she said in a low, menacing voice.

"I don't..." I began but fell silent as I looked at what was in her hand.

She was holding a small caliber, blue steel automatic pistol.

"None of you ever listens to me," she said as she pulled the trigger twice.

Twin shafts of fiery pain exploded in my abdomen. I looked at Melissa's hard face for a bewildered moment before I fell to the sidewalk.

I lay there on my side, holding my belly, feeling the sticky warmth of my own blood oozing through my fingers onto the pavement, staring dumbly at Melissa. The automatic clattered on the sidewalk when she dropped it. I heard her running footsteps as the great darkness descended upon me.

CHAPTER 9

S o I'm not dead, I thought. Without opening my eyes I knew that I was in a hospital. The air on my face was slightly chilly, there was that too-clean, too-sterile smell, and the intense light whose brightness registered through my shut eyes all typified hospital. I could both hear and sense a presence in the room, but I did not want to let anyone know that I was awake, not yet. A groggy muddle, no doubt caused by pain killer drugs, robbed my mind of the clarity it would need to face the inevitable questions for which I'm not sure that I had any real answers. The thought of playing 'possum in middle age forced an involuntary chuckle that gave me away.

"Are you awake, Mr. Farnigan?"

Conceding defeat I opened my eyes to look at the nurse, young, dark-haired and crisply efficient looking. Yes, indeed, I was not dead—I could not ignore that fact that she was very cute.

I nodded.

"How are you feeling?" she asked as she took my hand to take my pulse.

"Not dead."

She frowned. "It was close, Mr. Farnigan."

"How long have I been here?"

"Four days."

I nodded. The nurse was now bustling around my bed, checking the tubes and bottles that hung over it.

"Don't move your left arm around," she cautioned. "There are I.V.'s in it."

Not only there, I noticed. Tubes were everywhere—in my arm, my nose, and my privates. Wires had been attached to my chest to monitor my heart. There didn't seem to be much I was doing on my own.

A doctor appeared, summoned by telepathy or, more likely, an unseen signal from the nurse. It was the same doctor who had treated me a week or so ago. There was a look of mild disapproval on his face, I thought. He probably felt that if I had not walked out against his advice I wouldn't be here now.

The doctor gave me a full damage report. When you're gut shot at close range chances are never good. What had saved me was that Melissa's gun didn't really pack that much punch, relatively speaking. At the range I was shot at a .38 would have all but literally blown me in half. Melissa's gun was no near as powerful, still, it had done plenty of damage. I was glad I did not understand all the doctor talk, and I asked for no translation; but what was loud and clear was that I had almost died between blood loss, organ damage and the inevitable abdominal wound infection. A priest had read the last exit lines over me. The doctor promised me a long, slow recovery.

It wasn't until the next day that I finally had to speak with the police. A youngish inspector, named Jerry Chambers handled it in a matter of fact way. He asked routine questions, and I told him what had happened, omitting nothing. It was, after all, pretty simple. I had crowded Melissa and she had shot me for my trouble.

"That should be all," said Chambers as he gathered up his papers.

"I guess so—at least until you grab Melissa."

He said: "You don't know about it?"

I looked stupidly at him.

"Melissa Brinton is dead. Her body was found in Golden Gate Park three days ago. She had been strangled."

I spent a long time processing this, even as I realized I had pretty much expected it. Finally, I muttered, "Case closed."

"Probably," Chambers agreed. "It's not likely we'll ever catch her killer."

"No leads?"

"As cold a trail as you can get. Usually it's the pimp we'd be looking for, but not this time. He's dead, too."

"Real neat and tidy," I said bitterly.

"You've been around, Farnigan. You know how things are when certain people are involved."

"Yeah. Harry Salomon gets away with murder."

Chambers shrugged. "Salomon's just a taxpayer like you and me until we have something on him."

"Right."

"He'll screw up sometime. They all do."

"We all live in hope, Inspector."

After a few more words Chambers left, and I was alone with my tubes, wires, bottles and thoughts. That Melissa and Randy were both dead had an inevitability to it, yet it seemed so wasteful, so meaningless, to have two young lives snuffed out. I don't know where their lives went wrong, and maybe no one could ever know. It seemed to me, though, that something should have prevented them from becoming the playthings of Harry Salomon. I was thinking of how I would talk about all this to a priest friend of mine when sleep mercifully overtook me.

Only the removal of my tubes and wires made the next few

days eventful. I even managed to walk a few steps on my own. When I was allowed to have some Jell-O and a bowl of bland hospital broth for dinner, I was almost ecstatic. My closest friends visited, and they helped me through the depression that had fell upon me after Inspector Chambers' visit.

Another visitor was Estelle Brinton.

Some people can be elegant even in their grief, and Estelle Brinton was that as she stood by my bed. One thing about her was different. A permanent aura of sadness had closed around her, and she no longer retained any youthfulness.

"I'm so sorry, Bob," she said.

"I didn't lose a daughter."

"You almost lost your life." She wiped her eyes with a handkerchief. "She was lost a long time ago. I shouldn't have sent you after her."

"You had to, Mrs. Brinton. It would have been wrong to give up."

"I wonder about that. Maybe there are those times when you have to stand back and let things happen as they will."

"You don't believe that."

"No, I don't. I never have."

"Anyhow, Mrs. Brinton, the fault may have been mine. I don't think I mishandled it—but I'll always have some doubts."

"Tell me about that night," she said.

Estelle Brinton was not a person to lie to, to attempt to hide things from, and so she got the whole story. As I spoke she was impassive, only occasionally would her face begin to betray the agony she felt. When I was through, Estelle Brinton was pale and there was an uncharacteristic waver in her voice.

"Melissa was shooting me when she shot you," she whispered.

I nodded.

"I cannot understand such hatred."

"No one does, Mrs. Brinton."

She sighed. "Maybe it was my fault."

"I don't think so. Everyone—you, me, Melissa—has a dark side, the side that evil can appeal to, the side that will lead us away from all that we know to be right and good. There's something very seductive about evil, particularly if it's joined to the rebellion of youth. What was worse for Melissa was that she had a lot of wicked people in her life. Make no mistake, Melissa was trapped."

"Then why didn't she accept our help!" Estelle Brinton cried out in anguish.

"I don't know if you're religious, but I remember reading something about that by St. Augustine." I paused and she nodded for me to continue. "St. Augustine talked about the habit of sin, about how a person continues to do wrong even after it has lost all its attraction, satisfaction and desirability. He says that it becomes a thing-in-itself, with a life of its own—that the wickedness becomes an identity. St. Augustine offered only the grace of conversion as a way out."

"You're saying it was out of our hands."

"Yes, Mrs. Brinton, it was. What Melissa's life had become was beyond reach. But, dammit, we still had to try—it was our duty."

She rose. "You give me much to think about."

"I wish I could relieve you of your pain, Mrs. Brinton."

"Only time can do that. Words of comfort and all the niceties can do nothing. I do appreciate your care and thoughts from St. Augustine. There's not much comfort in them, but there is truth in them and, perhaps, I need that most of all."

Estelle Brinton walked over to my bed and took my free hand in hers.

"Please don't worry about your expenses, I'll be taking care of them. I know you have no medical insurance." I mumbled something, but she went on. "I owe you a lot for your help. You put your own life on the line for Melissa and me. I'll never forget what you tried to do for us. Thank you."

She squeezed my hand, turned, and left the room before I could say a word.

I never saw Estelle Brinton again.

CHAPTER 10

My recovery was uneventful. Good to her word, Mrs. Brinton was exceedingly generous in covering my medical expenses. She had also paid me well. I felt bad about taking her money considering how things turned out. But I needed it, which made me feel even worse.

I healed slowly and found it difficult to regain any energy. After being discharged from the hospital I spent the next six months in my tiny apartment doing nothing but reading, listening to music, and eating too much. It seemed as if something had been permanently altered in me, that I had become a stranger to myself. My few friends and the lady in my life were patient with me and left me mostly to myself, which was how I wanted it. They figured things would change when Mrs. Brinton's money ran out.

It didn't.

I began living on my meager savings. I gave up my office and made a deal with my landlady. My makeshift office, such as it was, was now in what had been her garage. She decided she'd like another monthly check more than the convenience of parking in it. That's cheap office space and I had no complaints, although a potential client expressed outrage when he slipped on a patch of oil on the concrete floor.

It kept the overhead down, I would tell them, and they did believe that.

The office wasn't much to look at. The old roll-top desk, my swivel chair, the file cabinet with the two drawers, and a canvas director's chair for the client. Not exactly impressive, but I would always move the car out when I knew a client was coming.

The latest client handed me a leaflet.

THANATOS NEW AGE MEDITATION AND BURIAL SOCIETY.

That's what the leaflet said. In smaller print was some kind of gibberish about the joy of death, the experience we've all been living for. Dr. Edmund Potter Stone, disciple of Sri Mareesh Pavantnantah, offered meditation, preparation, guidance, and a cheap burial. He had a temple and a crematorium in the lovely hills of Marin County for the use of the living and the dead. The living attended lectures and meditated; the dead went up in smoke.

I kept reading this over to avoid the intense stare of my client. She was about twenty-seven or so, tall, and rather lovely. I like skinny women. They aren't likely to have as deadly a punch as some of the big ones who have taken exception to being photographed by me. I'm paralyzed by the sight of a big, angry, naked woman bounding out of bed, vowing to rip my balls off. It's awesome. So I like skinny women, unless they know karate.

Not to worry about Kathy Adams. She appeared to be underfed. Kathy was almost boyish in her blue jeans and t-shirt, but her face was classically feminine and her little breasts (no bra) protruded quite nicely. Her gray eyes were, as I said, very intense, and eager.

I handed the leaflet back to her.

"So what," I said.

"Those are the people."

"Yeah. They brood about checking out and incinerate those who do." I leaned back in the chair. "Everybody dies." She was impatient.

"Of course people die, Mr. Farnigan."

"Call me Bob."

"People die, Mr. Farnigan, but I'm afraid ..."

"Of dying?"

"No." She paused. "Well, yes. Most of us are." She stood up. "You're not taking me seriously."

"I am, Miss Adams. Please, sit down and tell me everything." She sat and I continued. "After all, you walked in here, introduced yourself, and gave me that flier to read. It's a little ridiculous, you know. In fact, I began wondering if you weren't a salesman for this Thanatos outfit."

"I certainly am not, Bob." She was going to be friendly. "I'm worried about my Aunt and Uncle."

"Full names?"

"Juliet and Oscar Merton. Aunt Juliet is my mother's sister."

"Okay. What about the Mertons?"

"They belong to Thanatos."

"Are they old folks?"

"Sixtyish. Why?"

"It's a good age to be thinking about dying, that's all."

She lit a cigarette. "Uncle Oscar—we actually call him Uncle Skip—is obsessed about death."

"You call him 'Skip.' That's interesting."

"It's better than Oscar."

"Bob is better than Boris," I said.

She pondered this. "You name really is Boris?"

"Right."

"I see."

"You can say you're sorry if you like."

"No." She was cold and distant in tone.

I was irritating her. It's part of a financial death wish of mine: I tease my clients these days. I guess I hate my work. Her patience was all but gone. Time for seriousness.

"Miss Adams, you say Uncle Skip is obsessed with death. Has he been ill?"

"Oh no. On the contrary, he was very healthy ... before Thanatos. He only ate natural foods, he ran, he swam, and had no bad habits. I don't think I know anyone who was more dedicated to his own health and fitness."

"So we rule out bad health for him - at least initially."

"And for Aunt Juliet. She had never been sick a day in her life."

"Wish I could say the same."

"Me too," she laughed.

"Obsession with death doesn't seem to fit the picture."

"It's recent. Just in the last year or so. Since he found out about Thanatos."

"Uncle Skip is healthy, so he takes up death as hobby and gets unhealthy."

"Yes, his health is going." Not seeing an ashtray she absently put her cigarette out on the floor. "Aunt Juliet isn't doing well either. They both look dreadful—bony and tired—exhausted."

"Tell me, Miss Adams, what you think is going on." Another cigarette. I was going to have to buy an ashtray or fill a coffee can with sand.

"It's Uncle Skip's money. He's got quite a bit. He was a very successful stock broker on Montgomery Street before he retired."

"When was that?"

"Four years ago. I remember that he was just fifty-seven

then and he said that he wanted to do a lot of fun things before he died." She paused. "I think he was bored with his work. He was tired of commuting to San Francisco, the trips to L.A. and New York, everything."

She stared at the calendar on the wall for a while before continuing.

"He and Aunt Juliet did a lot after he retired. Skiing, a couple trips to Europe, and raising Pomeranians."

"Ugh."

"No kidding. They're nasty little dogs. I prefer cats," she added.

"Animals are a lot of trouble."

"I guess that's true, but they loved their dogs. Like a lot of childless people—Aunt Juliet had an ovarian cyst removed when she was very young—they used the pets for the children they never had." She shuddered. "That's what makes it so gruesome."

"What?"

"Four months after getting involved in Thanatos Uncle Skip killed all his dogs. He drowned them, one by one, in his hot tub."

"Christ."

"I never liked hot tubs, but now I can't stand the sight of them."

Kathy had turned a very unappealing pale green. I fumbled in my desk drawer for my thermos.

"I have some coffee here. Nothing stronger."

"Coffee would be fine."

I poured some coffee into a reasonably clean cup I found in another drawer.

"Here you go."

"It's not hot, Bob."

"Sorry. It's the morning's coffee."

"Never mind."

"You think I should move Mr. Coffee down here?"

"I think you should get a real office."

"This is just temporary." I lied. "I've been sick."

"I'm sorry. I'm a real bitch when I'm upset."

No arguing that.

She put the cup back on my desk and chain lit another cigarette. This time she thought of an ashtray.

"No ashtray either?"

"'Fraid not. Use the cup."

She did.

"The dogs were bad enough," she continued. "But there have been other things. They sold their home in Mill Valley and moved to a crummy duplex in Fairfax a few months ago."

"Why?"

"To be nearer to Thanatos. Thanatos has its temple or whatever in hills above Fairfax. Uncle Skip and Aunt Juliet spend most of their time up there."

"Anything else?"

"Uncle Skip seems to be divesting himself of all his assets. He told me that he was converting everything to cash."

"And you think the money is going to Thanatos."

"Of course." She stood up, angry. "They've become half-starved old people living in a four-room dump. All they do is talk about death, Thanatos, Doctor Stone and his goddamn guru. They're strangers now to the whole family. I want to know what's happening."

She sat, lighting yet another smoke. She had ground out the other one half finished.

"Have you been to the police?"

"Sure. I just got a lot of bullshit from them. No complaints on file, and all. The cop I talked to said that they can't investigate odd behavior. Unless there's a clear indication of criminal activity, they have to keep hands off nut groups. First Fucking Amendment rights."

She certainly was bitter. I wanted to ask her if she had lost out on any money thanks to the Merton's involvement in Thanatos, but I decided to save it for another day. She might just love the old folks; then again, she also might be an angry niece afraid of losing a once promised inheritance.

It was late afternoon now. I told her I would make some inquiries about Thanatos and that she should call me tomorrow in the early afternoon.

"You'll find out all about them, won't you?"

"What I can."

"I can't pay you much."

"Most of my clients can't, but your hundred bucks is a good start."

"Buy an ashtray."

CHAPTER 11

Kathy had gone and I locked the side door to the garage. One of the few conveniences of my life is that you can exit the garage directly into my apartment building's main hallway. It's a small thing, but I appreciate any break I get.

The building was once, apparently, a large single home—that was the reason it had only one garage. Some years back it was carved up into small apartments: two on the first floor, two on the second in the main part of the building. My place also was on the second floor, but it could be reached only by going out the back door on the main floor, and then up the outside stairs. If you continued up those same stairs, you'd reach a "penthouse" that had been constructed on the roof using what looked suspiciously like plywood. Period.

My apartment was ugly, bare and stale. The only beauty there was contained in my record collection. Music was my only real joy. It moved me deeply, removing any facades, allowing my soul to embrace the ineffable. Eclectic in taste, I am. I figure a mind usually in a state of muddle needed strong and different sounds. My collection was dominated by recordings of Bach cantatas and the extant works of Fats Domino. Johann Sebastian Domino? Fats Bach?

Once I was in tears after hearing Bach's Wachet Auf Cantata, and my landlady came to complain about the loudness of my private concert. She saw my swollen eyes, decided to say nothing, and walked away muttering about me needing a woman. I do. Maybe Anna Magdalena Domino would do just fine.

I wanted to forget about this Thanatos business. A feeling told me that this was really out of my league. I slink around smelly hotels with a camera; I'm not one to investigate extortion by ersatz gurus. But like I said, times were tough. Kathy Adams' hundred bucks was worth going through the motions. Cut rate detective; cut rate results. It was the way of the world.

A cynical bastard I am these days.

Just maybe, though, I would give it a try. Play at being a real detective. If nothing else the experience might make me more satisfied with my current place at the bottom rung of the business.

And make me forget Melissa Brinton.

I went to the icebox, resolved yet again to buy some food, and fetched a beer. I drank with shuddering satisfaction. Refreshed, I decided to telephone Larry Norton, aging San Francisco Gazette reporter.

Larry was there.

"Bob Farnigan, Larry."

"Long time," he wheezed.

"Still writing obits and fire calls?"

"Hell, no! I've been promoted back to municipal court. Of course, if anything interesting shows up they send down a boy with a good name."

He gave a bitter little laugh.

"It's easy work, Bob. And the bars around the Civic Center aren't too bad."

"You still get credit?"

Larry, with great dignity, said, "Sure. After all, I'm a professional. Bar tabs go with the turf."

"Look, I need a favor."

"If I can. Us old Jesuit schoolboys stick together."

I did not want any good old days bullshit so I rushed on. "Know anything about a nut outfit called Thanatos New Age Meditation and Burial Society?"

"Christ, that's a mouthful." He paused. "Yeah, I heard of it. Phil McGrath—you don't know him—came across them. Phil specializes in cults, radical groups and all that. He's a shithead."

"Did he get anything on them?"

"Nothing much. They never made any of his stories—too dull."

"Damn it."

"Sorry, Bob. All I remember is that Phil said that they were very big on dying with good karma. They get you keen on croaking and burn you cheap when you go."

"That's it?"

"Phil also said that their leader is a real creep. Didn't say why."

"That's not much help," I said. "I'm doing a little job right now. Some girl thinks her Aunt and Uncle are being taken by this bunch at Thanatos."

"Give more money and die better."

"I think that's it."

"You want I should ask Phil if he remembers anything?"

"I'd appreciate it. Tell him nothing is coming down yet—probably just a load of sour family grapes."

"But you'll let us know if you dig up anything fit to print?"

"Sure, I'd give you the story."

"That shithead McGrath would get the by-line."

"Too bad."

"It's okay," he said. "It would still be to my credit. God knows I need it around here." There was a silence as he consulted his own thoughts, then he laughed. "They keep me here as a warning to the kids."

We made some idle talk—good old days after all—and promised to get together with a bottle of Scotch soon, but we both knew we would not. Our friendship has been by telephone for years now.

Talking with one old acquaintance brought to mind another. I was overdue to pay a visit to my friend, Fred Morton. Fred had also grown up in the old neighborhood, the Richmond district of San Francisco. Unlike most of us he had made a successful attempt at higher things, including a sojourn as a history professor, a Medievalist. He never explained what had driven him away from his career, but I think a part of him regretted his departure from the academic cloister. In the years since he left the university he had devoted himself to eccentricity. Fred was a middle-aged man who wore work shirts and tie-dyed blue jeans, complained of bad teeth and took solace only in his wine, Gregorian chant, and writing letters. His letters flowed endlessly to Presidents, Popes, newspapers, and any person or organization that caught his irate attention. I liked to talk with Fred about everything, so I decided to call on him to discuss Thanatos.

Visiting Fred is easy. A walk halfway around the block. Thank God. Walking any distance near Russian Hill can be a steep, breath-robbing experience.

It was evening and I made good time to Fred's from my apartment. The late afternoon sun shone on the Bay Bridge, a bridge that was only beautiful when partially seen from a city street between the buildings.

Gregorian chant greeted my ears as I stood knocking at Fred's door. Then quiet as the monks were silenced and the door opened.

"Farnigan."

"That's me."

"Then come in. I've got a couple jugs of Chablis."

I removed Fred's cat, Chester, from a lumpy chair and settled in. Fred handed me a plastic water glass filled with wine.

"This wine has a powerful virtue," Fred announced. "It's dirt cheap."

"Last week was a vintage week."

"Precisely."

He ran his hand through his wildly wispy gray hair. I briefly told him about Kathy Adams and Thanatos.

"Greek," he said. "Thanatos is Greek for death."

"I remember, Fred. Eros and Thanatos always stayed in my mind."

"They go together."

"Like Stan and Ollie."

"Just not so funny."

He said, "It doesn't mix right."

"What doesn't?"

"This business about using a Greek word for death when the outfit allegedly follows an Eastern guru." He paused, musing. "Alexander the Great certainly brought thanatos to India when he visited them. Maybe a historically minded Swami is paying us back."

"Farfetched, Fred."

"Sure it is. But that's the nature of these fucking cults. Most of them are based on a little misinformation dangerously applied. Charlatans skim a little of the form, a few of the key words, and then muddle up innocent people. What's worse,

Farnigan, some of these frauds stumble upon dark forces that the truly wise never summon up or engage with."

"I think this Doctor Stone is just a crook."

"One can hope," Fred said. "God knows crooks do enough mischief. It's the meddlers with the occult who do the real evil, though."

I'm not much on dark forces and powers. Muggers and dope dealers are real enough for me. People can be real shits. Yet it is good to believe in the Devil. It makes reading twentieth century history easier.

"I'm sure I have a Bach cantata you don't own, Farnigan." Fred waved a record jacket at me.

"Hold it still, Fred."

He did.

"You're right. I don't have that one."

"Good. The hell with eros, thanatos and all that. Wine and Bach for us."

A pleasant evening.

CHAPTER 12

How I navigated home from Fred's that night is one of life's mysteries. It, too, shall be revealed. But, God, I hope not. Judging from my sore shoulder I must have fallen on the street at least once. Since I managed to get up and reach home I must not have been too drunk. Fred's bargain wines were always a source of devastation.

My hangovers are never fun. Light stabbed needle-like; sound pierced the swollen brain. My body was only reactive to more misery provided by hot bowels and bladder, a stomach trying to leap out. And, God, the regret. Stupid, self-destructive Farnigan had done it again.

Nothing worked that morning. No relief to be gained. The two beers I shakily drank were deposited in the toilet almost immediately and part of me longed for death. Yet another reaffirmed a desire to live. A belief that life was not bad itself, only a few moments here and there. Despite what others might say, I was essentially content with my life; but I no longer wanted to drink. That was it. No revelation or vow or anything. The time had come to retire my shot glass, to cease wrapping my lips around a bottle, at least 'til next time.

All this resolve did nothing for the hangover. Only time does that. So I still shook as I dressed, as I carved my face with the razor, and as I somehow managed to hold down a cup of coffee and a slice of rye bread. Part of me rejoiced in the new life just begun. A serenity crept over me. Boris "Bob" Farnigan —reformed drunk for today.

I made my way downstairs to my office. In a fit of fastidious-ness I collected the cigarette butts Kathy Adams had thought-lessly ground out on the floor. A man's office can be a dump but not a pig sty. Leaning back in my chair I began reflecting on Thanatos and a few brilliant conclusions faded as I fell into a heavy sleep. It was late afternoon when I awoke with a stiff neck. I had brought my usual thermos of coffee with me and it tasted wonderful now.

I phoned Kathy Adams.

"I wondered when you were going to call, Bob."

"I was busy."

"Oh, good."

"Nothing big yet. Just getting some background material. None of it helps with our problem. I do have, for what it's worth, assurance that Doctor. Stone is an asshole."

She was unimpressed.

"I could have told you that."

"True enough, Miss Adams." I paused. "I know you're at work and I don't want to tie you up. What I want you do to is phone the Merton's and arrange a visit. The two of us. As soon as possible."

"I don't know, Bob," she said. "I've hardly seen them lately myself. I don't know how they'll feel about a stranger."

"Tell them you're driving over that way with a friend on your way to a baseball game."

"There are no baseball games in Marin County," she interrupted.

"That's true enough. But there used to be a little Class A team in Sonoma County, and you have to go through Marin to get there. They might not know it's gone now."

"They probably don't know it ever existed, but going to Fairfax is about fifteen miles out of the way." She was adamant. "It's a lousy story. Anyhow, they know I despise baseball."

"I should have figured that."

We were both thinking now.

"Listen, Bob, let's try the truth. I'll tell them that I have a friend who may be interested in Thanatos. A shy guy who wants to hear about it indirectly before seeing Doctor Stone (the bastard)."

"That's an improvement over Class A baseball."

"Tell me about it," she said.

We disconnected. As I waited for her to phone back I was glancing through a copy of the diaries of Malcolm Muggeridge, a good man. He understood that there was a force other than gravity: the world sucked. Paradoxically, the world was also very beautiful. I guess a balance had to be struck between cynicism regarding the works of man and a faith in a redeeming God—a lot for a man with a hangover to think about.

Fortunately such theological speculations were cut short by Kathy's return call.

"It's all set," she said. "They'll see us anytime today."

Kathy was due to be off work in about an hour and we arranged to meet in front of the building she worked in. We would take my car.

I have previously alluded to my car. It's a heap. My eighteen-year-old car is a Chevy Impala, but I think Chevrolet would try to deny it if they saw it now. Dents, scrapes, scratches, and rusting metal covered the body. Inside, the seats were stuffed with newspapers and covered with serapes, but springs still attempted a swift, horrible castration from time to time. The rear floor and seat were filled with garbage. After all, what's easier than to throw empty cans, bottles, fast food wrappers, etc., into the rear? I never seem to get around to cleaning it out. However, let me say this: the car has a fantastic engine. Despite years of abuse and neglect, I have gotten over a hundred-fifty thousand miles out of it without any engine work being done. I think that has nothing to do with GM craftsmanship. The car is stubborn. It won't accept defeat.

The usual rush hour traffic confronted me in the financial district. For the thousandth time I thought of Will Roger's quip about the solution to the problem of heavy traffic being to limit driver licenses to those whose car was paid for.

Driving confirms me in my ever-growing misanthropy, believe me.

Kathy was standing at the corner of Geary and Stockton. She was wearing a subdued blouse and skirt outfit—tasteful and yet alluring. Ah, to be younger, slimmer, and less discouraged! No chance, Farnigan.

After a moment's shock at the sight of my car, Kathy got in. The asshole in the car behind me quit honking.

"My Volvo is in the shop."

Silence.

"I wish I had a Volvo," I said.

"I bet you do."

"This is a good car," I assured her. "It just looks like hell."

"It's filthy."

"Not really. Just cluttered. I'm usually too busy to attend to things like keeping the car clean."

"I doubt, Mr. Farnigan, if you're ever busy." She stared hard at me.

"I'm afraid you're right."

"Life hasn't been good to you, has it?"

"I dunno. Life's been all right—I just haven't reacted very well to it."

"I'm sorry," she said. Her stare had softened.

I asked, "Would you like your hundred dollars back? There are a lot more detectives in the phone book."

"I know that," she laughed. "I phoned a lot of them before you."

"But my price was right."

"Oh, that was part of it. I liked your voice, too." She was looking at the snarled traffic as the Golden Gate Bridge approached. "It's crazy, like this traffic, but I felt I could trust you."

"You can, Miss Adams."

"I believe you."

We rode silently across the bridge and into the hills of Marin. Until we started down Sir Francis Drake Boulevard toward Fairfax the only words she spoke were directions to the Merton's place. As we approached Fairfax, still in the strangling commute traffic, she began to speak of the Mertons, Uncle Skip and Aunt Juliet.

"They are good people."

"I'm sure they are."

"They are, you know. That's why I hate what's happening to them. It's like they're not alive already." She spat out the words. "God damn Doctor Stone!" Then she fell into a moment's silence. "I hope I'm right to butt in. They're adults. They have the right to live as they want. But I'm afraid for them."

"You should be."

"You really think so?"

"Damn right I do. You have no choice but to be suspicious. People, especially people entering old age, don't turn their lives upside down. It's a time to seek and maintain every goddamn bit of security you've got, not to turn your back on your whole way of living."

"That's what I believe, too."

"On the other hand, people their age have to face up to death. It's scary, you know. The active years are over, the body is slowing down, and the realization begins to dawn that time is now, in part, just a matter of waiting to die."

"You feel that way too?"

"No, I don't. I'm not that old, but I understand it. I've seen it."

"Your parents?"

"Among others. Some older friends, too. Nobody wants to cash in, especially if you're afraid that all everything has meant is reduced to a heap of rotting bones in a hole."

"Uncle Skip and Aunt Juliet were never very religious. Not a bit."

"So enter Thanatos. Last ditch salvation for the frightened."

"You can't call what is happening to them salvation."

"No, it's not. What it is, is a mixture of fear and promises. The good Doctor Edmund Potter Stone provides a mess of mumbo-jumbo to keep them confused and scared, sprinkled with some far-off promise of a way out. This, of course, requires their generous, free-will offerings to aid Doctor Stone in his work ... and buy them heaven."

"I'm sure that's what's hooked them."

"A regular church would have been cheaper."

"It's funny, Bob. They always thought all churches were a lot of bullshit."

"God is not mocked," I muttered.

By now we were in Fairfax and proceeding up Bolinas Avenue, My car was protesting the sustained steep grade. I think a little concern for the car was now also showing on Kathy's worried face.

"That's it."

Kathy pointed toward a duplex. It had been only a mediocre sort of building when it was built, probably early in World War II. The stucco needed patching and the cracked tile shingles needed replacing; the old place gave an impression of weariness, of too many years. The Farnigan Arms, I thought. An old age abode designed to make the grave more inviting.

After I had parked the car, we walked to the front door of the Mertons' rental sepulcher. Kathy touched my arm with surprising strength as I rang the doorbell.

"Be gentle," she said. "I do love them."

CHAPTER 13

Aunt Juliet opened the door. Next to me Kathy softly gasped. I could see why. No blue-haired Marin matron was Aunt Juliet. She was emaciated, veins sickly prominent; her short, gray hair pulled back into a severe parody of a ponytail. A shakiness in her voice copied the tremor that made her body seem vaguely out of focus. I irrationally recalled my elderly school teacher in the third grade: her veined, bony hand wielded a nasty ruler. I hated the old teacher; for Aunt Juliet I felt an angry pity.

"You have come with your friend after all, Kathy," she said, giving me a dubious look.

"This is Mr. Farnigan."

"Call me Bob, please."

"Come in. Mr. Merton doesn't like being alone." She paused. "Our Guide tells him that his needs must be overcome, you know."

"Doctor Stone is your Guide."

"Why, yes, Mr. Farnigan. However did you know?"

"I just guessed."

"You may be smart. Our Guide tells us that intelligence—

false intellect—is an impediment to liberation. You will profit if you follow that wisdom."

"I'm sure there is much for me to learn."

"There certainly is, and we must be thankful for a true Guide."

"I'm anxious to hear all about your Guide."

"Good," she said quite decisively. "But we must get in the house. There's a chill in the air."

A short hallway led to the living room. My flat is depressing enough, but it has signs of life at least. Not so, the Merton's apartment. The room was lit by a bare-bulb fixture, the sofa and three wooden chairs were of flophouse quality; no pictures, no plants or anything else relieved the bald tedium of the room. Other than the furniture the room held only a small pile of books near the sofa (one of which was the Tibetan Book of the Dead) and Mr. Merton, Uncle Skip himself, sitting on the sofa.

If Aunt Juliet had looked gauntly ill, Uncle Skip appeared to have already passed from sickness to death. I couldn't believe that he had ever been the hearty man Kathy had described. Call the grave diggers, I thought. No, I corrected myself, send him off to Thanatos' incinerator.

Uncle Skip was a cadaver with translucent skin and sunken eyes that did not seem to see. He had the pitiable frailness that large men have when wasting away. His voice, obviously once strong and deep, had a hollow, rasping quality. It was faint. This was more and more like a séance with genuine apparitions.

"So you're Kathy's friend." A skeleton-like hand rose up slowly from the seated Uncle Skip. Large bones and tight skin. No flesh. I could have crushed it with my flabby paw. Our hands barely closed on each other. The effort was exhausting for him. For a moment after the spectral handshake he sat in total, breathless silence.

Aunt Juliet had moved a chair behind me. I sat. "Kathy has

been telling me about Thanatos," I said. "About how it's changed your life."

"Oh, yes. It certainly has." He looked at Aunt Juliet who nodded. "Both of our lives have changed, mine and Mrs. Merton's."

"You have found a new way of living. I can tell."

"I'm sure it's obvious. A spiritual transformation has taken place. I am no longer a slave to my body, my ambitions and the dream that is maya—that's Sanskrit for the illusion that the material is real."

"I've read about maya."

"What?"

"The Bhagavad-Gita."

"Oh, that," he said contemptuously. "It is full of teaching that can lead one astray. Our Guide, Doctor Stone, and his Master, Sri Pavantnantah, have had to remove the impure teachings from the Gita and the Upanishads. The Vedantists have been great corrupters, you know."

"They have great influence, especially among Western intellectuals, Mr. Merton."

"Mind is rot; thought is death. Our Guide says something like that, only better. You get the meaning though."

"Thought is not to be trusted."

"Among other things, Mr. Farnigan."

"Call me Bob."

"Names don't matter. They only identify illusions."

"I like Bob, anyhow."

"As you wish."

"I would like to know more about the Guide and the Master."

"In a moment." He made a slight gesture to Aunt Juliet who rose and left the room. "Mrs. Merton will get us some tea. It's our evening sustenance."

"You are on a strict diet, it seems."

"Food feeds an illusion. We eat only enough to maintain ourselves until the time comes when the illusion has been overcome."

"And then?"

"We die."

With that cheerful conclusion the tea arrived. It was weak and watery, served in water glasses. My fingers were going to be blistered. The wreck of Uncle Skip stared at my scalded fingers. I guess the old man wanted to see if the Farnigan illusion experienced pain. It did. But the only clue was, I think, the sweat that burst out on my forehead.

"Simple needs only," he said as he sipped the tea. "We cannot afford the complex."

"It would interfere with your purification, wouldn't it?"

"Of course it would."

"The road to heaven can't be found with Julia Child's cookbook."

"I detect a certain facetiousness, Mr. Farnigan," he said severely, glaring at me and Kathy.

"I am flawed, Mr. Merton."

"We all are—except our Guide and his Master, of course. At least you are beginning to seek the Truth."

"I am, Mr. Merton. That's why when Kathy told me about you, I asked if I could visit." I continued humbly, "I thought it best not to bother a great teacher like Doctor Stone, but to find a fellow seeker."

"Doctor Stone will see anyone, no matter how degenerate in the ways of illusion."

(Thanks a lot, old fart, I thought.)

"You could have gone easily to our ashram."

"It's near here, I understand."

"Just down the road a few miles. Up in the hills. Mrs. Merton and I walk out there daily."

He said that defiantly. I think even he realized that their going any distance on foot had to evoke images of a medieval dance of death. I must have looked incredulous.

"We discipline our bodies, but we find the strength to pursue our path of liberation."

He said, "We eat two cups of rice a day and drink some tea although we do fast from time to time. When not working and praying at the ashram we are meditating at home. Mrs. Merton and I no longer sleep more than four hours a night. All our time is needed to find enlightenment and liberation before it is too late this time."

"This time?"

"This life, of course. We are fixed on the wheel of karma, an endless cycle of death and rebirth. Through the teachings at Thanatos we can finally die and become One."

"Thanks to Thanatos you overcome death." I spoke as an avid disciple.

"Death becomes our finest hour if we have conquered illusion." A fearful look came over him. "But if we die unenlightened, the damnation is horrible, beyond imagining. We revert, if damned, to the lowest order of life form, and we have to progress through myriad rebirths up the ladder of evolution to a chance, as a human, for salvation again. I once thought that death was a great nothing, but now I know enough to realize its full horror if a soul is not prepared."

"Doctor Stone has taught you all this?"

He nodded, still somewhat horror-struck by death's finality.

"Let me ask you this: how did you meet Doctor. Stone?"

"What a curious question, Mr. Farnigan. It was part of my predestined experience."

"I appreciate that, but I would like to understand the workings of predestination." I was insistent. "How did you meet Doctor Stone?"

"Very well. Destiny moves in simple channels. It was a mutual acquaintance, a man whose investment portfolio I had once handled. Richard Kelland was his name. He introduced me to Doctor Stone." He shook his head with sadness and vehemence. "But he has since renounced his chance to achieve liberation."

"He left Thanatos?"

"He is a pariah. An untouchable who has dared to blaspheme. Richard Kelland not only questioned that teaching, he also made vicious accusations regarding our Guide's integrity."

"What kind of accusations?"

"I hate to spread falsehood, Mr. Farnigan...Bob. Yet I detect in you the signs of one in search of truth. So I'll demonstrate the ways of folly and illusion. Richard Kelland said that Doctor Stone, our Guide, was nothing more than a con man." He leaned forward and put his quavering hand on my knee. "Richard Kelland did not have the strength of soul to relinquish his worldly goods forever. He said that our Guide had impoverished him; the truth is our Guide had sought to lead him to the enrichment of eternal enlightenment. Richard Kelland is a weak, evil man."

"I don't quite understand why he would have said that Doctor Stone had impoverished him."

"Quite simple actually, Mr. Farnigan. When Richard first told me of Thanatos, it was when he was liquidating his worldly possessions. As his former counselor, I was asked to help. Unenlightened as I was, I had a skeptical attitude towards Thanatos; I was, I'm sorry to say, suspicious of Richard's signing over most of his wealth to Thanatos. In fact, I insisted on meeting with Doctor Stone. His insight and spirituality convinced me that Richard had found a good thing." He stood up. "I met our

Guide and I soon began the road to a new life—the new life death will bring. I, too, renounced my possessions."

Uncle Skip was now standing next to Kathy who had been sitting on another chair next to me. There was an avuncular fondness in the ruined man's manner. Kathy was quite moved.

"There were some things I never told you about, Kathy."

"What were they, Uncle Skip?"

"Your Aunt and I have had some illness we never mentioned to you."

Kathy gasped and took his frail hand in hers.

"You know how old couples get more and more alike, don't you? Well, we both have heart disease—angina, they call it. Angina isn't fatal in itself, but it bodes of trouble to come."

"I'm so sorry," Kathy said. She kissed his hand.

"Don't worry, Kathy." He stroked her hair with his free hand. "We have overcome our own fears. We were afraid, you know. But no longer do we fear at all."

Kathy's eyes had filled with tears. She was unable to speak the words her trembling lips formed. Uncle Skip, shell of a man, became her comforter.

"There, now, don't be sad," he soothed. "We will be fine, now and forever."

They communed in silence. And when the moment passed, Uncle Skip, with a sudden briskness, ended our interview. He urged me to seek Dr. Stone, to learn at Thanatos. It was an invitation to die too soon.

CHAPTER 14

Once back in my hobbled chariot Kathy began to cry, painful sobs from innermost grief. I was helpless. My futility in being able only to hold her shaking body angered me. I, too, hate illusions, the ones that evil men use to distort and maim the foolish or the afraid. A hardened voice in me suggested that the Mertons were moral weaklings who deserved their agony. You know the voice: the one that dithered about being free, white and twenty-one. But that voice was overridden by the sound of Kathy's tearing sobs. Maybe the Mertons didn't matter (they were, after all, big folks); but the poison of Thanatos, metastatic, spread to the wholly innocent. And, yes, hadn't the Mertons been caught in its widening pool of venom?

Boris Farnigan is no hero. Honesty requires that I admit to a disproportionate share of human cowardice. I was once hit by a car while running away to avoid a fight I probably could have won. Yet, despite these craven credentials, I had made Thanatos and its bogeyman Guide my sworn enemy.

Brave words, Farnigan. Now, do something about the crying girl, I thought.

It is easier, you know, to plot horrid revenge in lurid, wide screen imagination than to deal with basic human pain.

"Don't worry," I said feebly. "We can do something to help."

Sobs.

"I know crying helps. But we have to get going. I don't want them to look out and think that something is wrong."

She nearly gagged repressing a sob. "You're right. Take me home."

We drove in silence except for street noises and Kathy's assaults on my handkerchief—the only clean one I owned. Like its predecessors, once used, it would vanish from my life into the garbage pail, for I have a fetish that no soiled snot-rag can ever become hygienic again.

I glanced at the young woman from time to time. Kathy Adams was indeed another Farnigan poverty case. It figured. She worked at a medical supply firm and since health-care funding to the ailing poor was in flux, Kathy spent her days calling people with respiratory illnesses. Her company was repossessing the oxygen equipment the state had been paying for. Cheerful work and Thanatos, too. Her pay was minimum meager, hence, Kathy Adams lived in a rundown apartment building on the edge of the formerly hip Haight-Ashbury district.

I offered to see her to her apartment, but she refused. She made a wretched attempt to smile and in silence walked up the cracked concrete steps.

I felt like a used bedpan in a cholera clinic.

Filled with scatological thoughts and dreams of vengeance I drove to a nearby liquor store. To my own surprise I passed up strong drink. I bought four candy bars, two pieces of over-processed alleged summer sausage snack, and a large bottle of mineral water. That was dinner. That was more refuse for the Chevy's backseat.

The shock of so much sugar and greasy pig meat had outraged my entrails and deepened my depression. I needed companionship. No, not Fred Morton, for that was the road to a hangover. I decided to see my sometimes conscience: Father Daniel Brendan Fahey.

Yes, it's trite. I know it is. But if you are raised in an Irish Catholic neighborhood and go to parochial school, at least one of your friends gives up the Devil for the priesthood. Dan had done so late in life—in his early thirties; he had what used to be called a delayed or late vocation. His wife and kid had died in an auto wreck and his pious instincts had taken over as a consequence. Dan was a big man with a prominent nose disfigured by drink and numerous breaks. He had pursued the other hackneyed Irish career: he had been a fireman. A goddamn tough one who also had a great Golden Gloves boxing record. Now he drank sacramental wine only, fought with Satan exclusively, and nurtured a hatred for Vatican II. Dear Lord, he would lament, are they trying to make the Church the largest Protestant denomination in Christendom? Best not to agree too vehemently, though. Dan tolerated no hint of disrespect for the Church.

Anyhow, I found myself knocking at the rectory door with an aching stomach and a morbid mind. It seemed appropriate to be at the Via Dolorosa parish.

Father Daniel Brendan Fahey opened the door himself. "God be praised," he said drolly. "All I need is another sinner. Come in."

We passed through the office into Dan's living quarters. "Have a seat."

"With pleasure."

"Too much pleasure if you ask me," he said scornfully. "You've got a gut and a butt that's starting to defy the laws of gravity."

"I always had a big ass, Dan. You called me 'Bob Barnbutt' when we were kids."

"You got the whole farm now, Farnigan."

"Farmer Farnigan, at your service." After a chuckle, I asked, "How is the priest business?"

"You'd be scared of the ferocious stuff I hear in the box. But not enough of them are in there these days. No goddamn guilt anymore."

"They'll come around."

"I hope for that," he sighed. "The world's changing. My parish has a lot more Latinos coming in now. The bishop suggested I learn Spanish to say Mass for them."

"Your accent will be lousy."

He contemplated his language problem for a moment. "You didn't come for parish gossip."

"I didn't. But I find it hard to start talking about it."

"Try my patience and start at the beginning, Barnbutt."

I did. Father Daniel Brendan Fahey was a good listener, and except for some expressions of outrage as my story progressed, he never interrupted.

"This case is too much for me," I concluded.

"It's a bad one for sure."

"I would give it up if I didn't feel obliged, if I wasn't so goddamn mad."

"Don't blaspheme, Farnigan."

"You do."

"We are all sinners. But I'm paid to tell you, you are."

"I'm a sinner who has a duty to a client I'm supposed to help. She's a good kid."

"You're not confusing horniness and duty, are you?"

"She would only laugh."

"Women are funny ones. Remember that."

"Dan, believe it or not, I've had an attack of idealism."

Father Fahey made a face. He had always had grave doubts about any person's self-avowed idealism. One of his favorite comments was that fine words and thoughts usually are trying to disguise a grab for the nuts. This bit of wisdom was, I believe, cleaned up in his homilies. Maybe not.

"Listen, Farnigan," he said in his most authoritative manner. "You're dealing with scum. This heretic Stone is not only lining his own pockets, he's doing the Evil One's work. He's presenting a perverted version of religion. Mind you, I think the turban and loincloth boys have but a small inkling of what our Faith has revealed, but that doesn't make what he's doing to Eastern wisdom less evil. The man is interfering with God. He is using the natural thirst of man for God to dominate, destroy and pervert.

"I'll give you advice, Farnigan. Go to that Thanatos sewer. Dig up all you can. For God's sake be subtle, though. If you are to unravel this, you'll have to catch them at it. Stone may not have obviously broken any law yet—but I doubt it. You have to learn enough about Thanatos to be able to at least scare him off, and get him off the backs of people like the Mertons."

By this time Dan was marching around the room. I had visions of him questioning Dr. Edmund Potter Stone with the aid of a rubber hose. I could imagine Dan's earnest expression of regret for Stone's unfortunate but clumsy accident at the station house. Too bad Dan had never been in the cop business.

"Remember," he said when he sat again, "Don't force his hand. Sweet talk him. Be a sincere seeker of his infernal guidance. Con the con man, Farnigan."

He added, "I'll be praying against him."

"God and Farnigan versus Stone and Thanatos."

"I have some faith in you, Farnigan. Although I will save most of my faith for Our Lord."

"That's your job."

"Not that I wouldn't mind having a chance at this Thanatos bullshit."

"You're a great help as it is."

"Once a fighter always a fighter."

"It's true, you know."

"I suppose you have a point." He shook his head. "I really wish that it wasn't so. A priest is what I am, not an instrument of earthy retribution."

My chance to reassure a priest: "You are a good priest, Dan."

"I don't see you at mass, Farnigan."

"I have problems."

He said, "So you're still seeing Elizabeth."

"Yes."

"I bet she goes to Mass."

"She does. But not communion," I added.

"You would go to Mass if your, ah, irregular ways didn't keep you from the sacraments, but you won't give up your sin."

"That's about it."

"You stubborn sinners are the worst of the lot."

"You love the challenge."

He said, "Get out of here, now. Do your work! At least some of it is God's own."

"Goodnight, Dan."

As I left, he stood at the open rectory door and I was aware that he was making the sign of blessing over me. I was thankful.

CHAPTER 15

M arin County again. I was driving out Bolinas Avenue from Fairfax. The road is fairly steep, and once past the homes along the roadside the terrain becomes more rugged —hills, trees and tall brown grass. Unless you're immured in the blinding maze of the Los Angeles megalopolis, California offers the opportunity to escape from city to nature with comparative ease, almost at will. Part of the schizoid perversity of California lies in this duality: part virgin landscape and part polluted center of urban decadence. I wouldn't trade it for the world, believe me.

While pondering all this in order to avoid the matter at hand, I almost missed the narrow dirt road marked by a crude handwritten sign that merely said Thanatos Ashram. My car is an eyesore, but the brakes are good and I emerged from my self-made dust storm and began up the road. The road was deeply rutted, my shock absorbers woefully inadequate, and I was thankful not to be hung over today. It amazed me that the Merton's ruined bodies could tolerate their daily walk out to their Guide because it was all uphill through low trees until the ashram itself, built on a surprising stretch of flat ground, came into view. A bizarre view. The crematorium was away from the main building near where the trees began again.

I thanked God that no smoke was visible. For late twentieth century tastelessness, though, the ashram was an epitome. It had obviously once been a white stucco ranch house; now, however, ersatz towers had been added on and the middle of the roof was dominated by a large representation of a radiant sun made of gold painted metal. Worse, the walls had amateurish paintings on them of Hindu deities waving their multiple arms and legs in what was, presumably, a dance of life through death. If God was of the Hindu persuasion, all connected with this travesty were in eternal trouble.

There appeared to be no particular pecking order for parking, so I let the Chevy expire at the first reasonable place. Only about four other cars were in sight. I didn't want to go to the grotesque building, rather, I wanted a drink in a saloon far away. Here I was, though, sweating in my car, my duty to do. Part of me was still sufficiently outraged to want to pursue this case, but I was also assailed by doubt: can a motel photographer be of any use in this place?

Probably not.

Without warning old memories flooded over the present and suddenly a part of me mourned for the amusement arcades of my youth—the mechanical laughing lady, the smell of over-steamed hot dogs, and the bells and lights of the pinball machines. I thought of No Nose Nolan who, drunk, had walked over to a parked cop car and peed on it; I remembered sneaking a peek down Mary Teresa Flynn's blouse and discovering she really had tits; and I recaptured the young Bob Farnigan who just wanted to hang out. Perhaps the first ambitions are the right signs of vocation. It was possible that Fate intended nothing more for me than to be a full-time idler, drinking brew, having a succession of bleached old ladies and earning a living doing odd jobs for buddies, or some occasional fencing.

Nostalgia for a different way of failure.

I wanted no part of this present, but right then I was too hot to continue sitting in the car that was still wheezing in a near terminal rattle—there was nowhere to escape to. Thanatos was all there was.

"Welcome, friend," a voice said as I got out of the car. A medium tall man with amiably Slavic features and too blissful eyes held out his hand. "The name's Ralph."

"Mine's Bob," I said as we shook hands.

"You come to see our Guide?"

"That's right. He around?"

"Whether here or there he's with us. I don't know if you get me, but what you got to know is that the Guide's teachin' is what counts."

"That's what I want to find out, Ralph."

He said, "You come to the right place."

Christ, I thought, a happy cretin.

"Yeah," he continued, "if you got troubles with livin', you got to learn about dyin'."

"The Guide says that?"

"Something like that. The important thing is to be here, to open up the brain to hear the words."

Ralph wasn't as emaciated as the Merton's, but it looked like a plate of spaghetti and a couple of steaks wouldn't hurt him. Judging from his hands he was a man used to hard work, but his brain wasn't.

I asked, "Why did you come here?"

He gave a wonderfully open and naïve smile. He wanted to tell his story.

"My life was a mess. I drank too much, I hit the wife, and I stole money from the neighbor's house. You know, the neighbors always kept the money in the same drawer. They never learned, I guess. I don't know about you, but I thought that sort of stuff wasn't too good for me."

I agreed and he continued.

"So I drank and stole and whacked the wife. She was always mad at me, yelled at me, you know. Don't get me wrong, I love my wife and since I come here I haven't had to hit her. Actually, I don't see her much no more. Funny thing, I quit drinkin', I quit stealin' and I stopped hittin' her—but she leaves me mostly alone anyhow. I don't know about you, but women don't make no goddamn sense."

"Even Freud wondered what women really want."

"That I don't know. What I do know is that Molly likes me less now that I stopped being a shit."

"After you came here?"

"Yeah. My whole life changed."

"You got religion?"

He shook his head.

"Religion I don't have. It's a spiritual way of life I have. I was a Catholic once, though."

"You left the Church?"

"A long time ago. When I was young. Religion didn't do it for me. It pissed me off when the brothers belted me one when I couldn't subjugate a Latin word."

"Conjugate," I said pedantically.

"That's it," he said. "See how little I got out of religion? Anyhow, when my life became a mess—you know, drunk and all that, Molly pissed off, my business going to hell—I tried the Church again. I went to the church and I stood at the front of the place, and I told God that I didn't like the Church. I told Him if He wanted me to be a Catholic He would have to tell me so, but He didn't say a damn thing. So I haven't been to church since."

"I can understand that," I said.

"Then you've come to the right place."

I looked around. There was still no sign of anyone else. "Tell me, Ralph," I said, "is the Guide inside now?"

"That he is. I think he's meditating, or maybe he's asleep. It's a hot day."

A glimmer of an excuse to get away overcame me.

"Maybe I shouldn't bother him today, Ralph."

"No, you don't understand. He's here to be bothered." Ralph turned toward the mythic manor and began walking. "I'll take you to him."

I was stuck.

Ralph was quiet as we walked to the entrance, the only sound was that of the dust and gravel crunching under our feet. A part of me wanted to avail itself of this last opportunity to escape the madness of Thanatos—after all, the car should have recovered from the journey by now. But, no, my legs brought me and my ambivalent mind through the entrance.

Inside the same ugliness that characterized the exterior prevailed, although muted by the weak light of a few discreetly placed track lights and myriad candles. Again there were garish depictions of Hindu deities, but the assault on the eyes was nothing compared to the stench of incense that permeated the room. I suppose a former altar boy should not object to incense, but this one had a peculiar and strange scent—far too acrid, sweet, and heavy. My eyes watered; my nostrils burned.

Through tears and dimness I could make out several people in the room. One was an elderly man seated on a cushion along a side wall. As usual around here, he was painfully thin and had a look of desperate ecstasy. Maybe the incense had made him high. The other person, also a man, was seated on an overstuffed cushion in front of the altar. His back was toward me, but he appeared to be enrapt in contemplation of the simple wooden altar. Statues of various deities stood on the garland laden altar. Behind the altar on the wall was a painting of a multicolored sun surrounded by innumerable spirit bodies.

"That's our Guide," Ralph whispered to me.

"Doctor Edmund Potter Stone himself?"

"The same," said Ralph.

"Sri Mareesh Pavantnantah isn't here, is he?"

"No. He stays in India."

"It surprises me that there is no picture of Sri Mareesh," I said as I glanced around to be sure that there was no picture.

Ralph said, "His picture is only displayed on his birthday."

"Makes sense, I guess."

"I don't know about you, but I think that when a holy man says what is the best time to show his picture, you gotta believe it's right."

We had been talking too loudly, I guess, because the skin and bones old man was hissing at us. This provoked the Guide's interest, forcing him to face us.

"Who is our guest, Ralph?"

"The name is Farnigan. Boris Farnigan—call me Bob."

"That's right, Guide," said Ralph.

"Come closer, Mr. Farnigan. Sit on this cushion next to me." Looking at Ralph he said, "You may go now."

Ralph mumbled and left.

I made my way, a few leaden steps, to sit at the right hand of the Guide. Under the force of my weight the cushion was defenseless: I could feel the cool hardness of the concrete floor. Doctor Edmund Potter Stone was silent and his detached manner forbade speech. So I studied the Lord High Charlatan. He was tall and thin, but well fed. Stone appeared to be in his late fifties or so. His face had few lines or wrinkles, and he had retained carefully trimmed sandy hair flecked with gray. Except for unexpectedly thick lips the face was lean and sharply defined.

"Have you finished analyzing my character, Mr. Farnigan?" he asked suddenly. His voice was cool, soft and engaging. "Can't judge a book by its cover."

"Quite right."

"My mother always said that, you know."

"I'm sure she would have."

"She did, Mr. Farnigan. But fascinating as reminiscences of mothers may be, I need to know why your mother's son is here."

"I know the Mertons," I said.

"They are good people, true souls seeking enlightenment and liberation." He said this almost casually, but grew more pointed as he continued. "How do you know the Mertons?"

"I really only just met them, but I know their niece. She talks a great deal about their experiences here."

"The niece is not, I believe, sympathetic to the way of life her aunt and uncle have found."

I could sense suspicion now as he looked intensely at me. "She doesn't understand higher things, Doctor Stone. Kathy— that's her name—thinks that religion is a refuge for the feeble minded." I laughed. "I wonder how she tolerates me."

"Perhaps she thinks you feeble minded, Mr Farnigan."

"I am a spiritual person. She distrusts that."

"Nonetheless she talks to you about the life of the spirit."

"That's right. At least, sometimes she does. I guess she likes me in spite of it."

"Enough of her," he said with a dismissive flourish of his hand. "What can I do for you?"

"You can help me, Doctor Stone."

"I am, of course, here to serve." He sounded dubious.

"Much help, Doctor Stone."

God does answer prayers, you know. He moved Dr. Stone to

suggest that we adjourn to his office so as not to disturb the atmosphere of meditation in the sanctuary. My aching legs and numbed butt rejoiced as I followed Stone through a side door into his office. Skeleton man in the sanctuary gave me a hiss as I closed the door.

CHAPTER 16

Stone's office was dominated by a large mahogany desk and a generously stuffed reclining chair. The lone chair for visitors was more spartan and barely accommodated me. Books with esoteric titles were shelved along one wall; the other wall was almost entirely a picture window that allowed a view of the wooded hill behind the ashram. I noticed a large safe in one corner behind Stone's desk. No doubt a repository for spiritual treasures not meant for the unredeemed.

"I would offer you refreshment, but my attendant is busy. Also, our interview may not last long enough to warrant amenities," he added smugly.

Time to grovel. Stone was no fool, he seemed suspicious and he had not liked mention of the Mertons.

"I'm eager and appreciative of any time you can give me, Doctor Stone. I know it must be a burden to have strangers coming to seek wisdom from you, but there are so few teachers—so few Guides."

"It is an easy burden. My own hope for liberation is in fulfilling the duty."

"I want to know more about Thanatos."

"Why?"

"You see me, Doctor Stone. I don't look healthy. I'm not. In fact, ill health ended my career as a teacher. For the last years I have been idle in terms of work, but my time has been spent seeking after higher things."

Stone's monetary sense was touched. "That's unfortunate, Mr. Farnigan. I presume you have been living on some sort of disability benefit."

"I get one of those. But I'm more fortunate than many. A great aunt left me a great deal of money."

The avaricious bastard repeated, "A great deal of money?"

"Yes. You know, I suppose some people would have spent it all on worldly pleasures, having fun with the time they have left. Not me. I live simply, almost like a down and outer. I need little for myself—for my body, that is. What I do need is hope and faith and a chance to return to the Light."

"Worthy, spiritual hopes, Bob."

"Thank you, Doctor Stone."

He leaned back in the chair. His manner became one of detached enlightenment and spirituality. In a moment he would launch into a sermonette on how to save my soul and dispose of my putative money. "Thanatos is, as you may know, the ancient Greek word for death. Although I carry the teachings of the most holy Sri Mareesh Pavantnantah from the East, I wanted to demonstrate the universality of his message by using a word from the cultural foundation of the West. The Orphic Mysteries of the ancient Greeks sought meaning, higher, mystical meaning, in the great mystery of thanatos—death."

"I see."

"Good," he nodded approvingly. "What the elders of our civilization sought to become initiated in, I have brought from the East."

"From your holy guru."

"Precisely. For many years I studied at his ashram, fasting and praying, until Sri Mareesh at last took notice of me and urged me to bring his teaching to America. I resisted, Mr. Farnigan. I did not want to leave my Teacher." A look of martyrdom passed over his face, followed by one of exalted resignation. "But one cannot ignore one's dharma, the duty of karma. If I am to achieve any escape from the burden of life and death it is through doing my guru's work.

"I have been laboring for some years now. At first I went from town to town, renting auditoriums, to spread Sri Mareesh's teachings. But I was led to establish this ashram. Here we only seek to attract by our example of meditation and our devotion to the needs of all who must die."

Nodding eagerly like a demented shill I said, "You care for the spirit and provide last services for the body. It's wonderful work."

(Translation: You rob, starve and then burn your suckers, you bastard.)

"You understand well, Bob. Of course, the care of the dead is the least we do. It is important that the proper rituals are performed for the dead, but the real work is with the living so that death holds no terror."

"That is the work of your teaching."

"Sri Mareesh's teaching," he corrected.

"I'm sorry."

"I am only the holy guru's agent. He teaches that we must prepare for death. By that he means a program of meditation, strict diet and a giving up all earthly goods. I have pamphlets on the course of meditation and diet to be followed. I also give weekly lectures on the methods to discipline mind, body and spirit. There are also the daily meditations that I lead every noontime."

"I'm sure I could follow that."

A look of profound sadness now overcame Dr. Edmund Potter Stone.

"Eager words, Bob. Sadly there is one great obstacle. Worldly possessions. So few are willing to give them up. It makes no difference for souls immersed in materialism that there is a path to a higher life, that death can be without fear, that in death all the cherished hopes of love and attainment can be achieved. No, Mr. Farnigan, not all men are willing to renounce that part of their lives."

Mr. Farnigan again—he had expelled me from the fold. "But Doctor Stone," I protested, "I already live a life that is simple; I have renounced all but the bare basics."

He glanced with some disbelief at my bulging belly.

"I know I look fat, but it's my illness. A metabolic disorder that sooner or later will develop into a cancer that will eat my fat body alive." I lied while making a note to consult the Merck Medical Dictionary to find a name for the disease I had described.

The bastard asked, "What is your disorder?"

"It has a funny name. I'm going to die and the name of my disease is even too much for me to pronounce."

"Cause of death is unimportant; what is crucial is that we are prepared. True preparedness through renunciation of the material world is the goal of Thanatos, Mr. Farnigan."

Still the surname.

"What good are my possessions when I'm dead? I'm dying, Doctor Stone, and it scares me. To find peace with death, I would gladly give away everything I own."

Flat eyes absorbed this. "You would receive guidance for doing that, Bob."

With all innocence, "I could, Doctor Stone?"

"Indeed, yes. There are ways your goods could be put to use to further the work and provide for your basic bodily needs." He feigned disinterest. "But that comes later. One must begin with the Teaching. Renunciation comes as one follows the Path."

"But my worldly goods could help your work?"

"Yes. There are trust funds from endowments to the Thanatos Foundation," he said patiently. "But that is a subject for a later discussion which we will have soon—if you choose to follow the Path."

He looked at his watch. It was a Rolex. "I regret that I have an appointment in San Francisco in about an hour and a half. I'm going to give you some of our literature, including the diet plan. Read it carefully. Try meditating on it. Begin the diet soon as you can. It is a very rigorous diet and you will suffer some initial discomfort, but it will pass and the diet's benefits will begin. If you do not like what you read, please do not reject it out of hand. Rather, come and speak with me again. You will read about the promises of the Life Eternal and, I think, you will want to follow the Path, Bob."

Dr. Edmund Potter Stone was giving a very professional bum's rush. He quickly grabbed a thin book and a number of tracts which he gave me, imploring me to read and follow them. He said he would accompany me to my car, and we left the office.

As I stood by the side of my car which had obviously appalled Stone, I reasserted my desire for simplicity and renunciation to the Guide. The car was good evidence of my sincerity.

The sound of a powerful automobile engine interrupted these valedictory pleasantries. It was a chauffeur-driven Mercedes Benz limousine. As it passed us, I could tell from the look on Stone's face that this was his so-called appointment in San Francisco. The man in the back seat was by the window nearest Stone and me. I recognized him, and my hands began to sweat. His face evidenced nothing but vacant disdain.

"Who's that?" I asked. "He looks familiar."

"I doubt you know him. Good day." Without further word, Stone turned from me and began walking to the Mercedes which had parked near the main building. When he reached the parked Mercedes he turned towards me, his gaze harsh.

I left.

No doubt Dr. Edmund Potter Stone and Harry Salomon had something private to discuss.

CHAPTER 17

The long drive back to San Francisco was uneventful, I think, but I'm not a trustworthy source for that. My mind was so overloaded with the facts and personalities of the case that I had no gray cells available for registering anything else. I might have taken notice if the Golden Gate Bridge had collapsed beneath me, but I could be wrong. A proof that I was both preoccupied and benumbed was that I didn't experience my usual bridge phobia. The Golden Gate Bridge is probably the most publicized location in America as a place for despondents' last leap into adventure. I'm basically too craven to contemplate suicide, but I do have this fear that my car will finally expire on the Bridge and, having nothing else to do, I will hop on over the rail. Whether or not this recurrent fantasy indicates a latent suicidal bent or merely a grossly exaggerated fear of the auto mechanic's repair bill is something I do not know.

Anyway, I arrived back in San Francisco and parked my car in the office. On the stairs up to my flat I met the landlady who told me Larry Norton had been to see me. Shit, I thought, I'll have to telephone him and talk about Thanatos. My lips ached with the desire to attach themselves around a bottle. A cut-rate detective should not attempt to sober up while he is in over his head. Oblivion would be better. Get drunk, stay drunk until fired, and then go back to the safer, sleazier way.

Poor Kathy Adams, I thought. Some hero.

Inside the flat the air was stale and weary as I sat in the kitchen eating potato chips and drinking lemonade. I glared at the sliced salami that had withered and turned rancid in the refrigerator, forcing me into this vegetarian diet. As a measure of my despair I considered going to see Elizabeth in hopes of a real meal. She would feed me and maybe share her bed again with me, but I would feel like shit.

Father Dan Fahey, I thought, is ruining my life. He has managed to stir up all my guilt about Elizabeth Casey.

Elizabeth is another relic of my youth, a childhood sweetheart before she went to the nunnery. After a few years, she left the Little Sisters of the Holy Shroud, and for reasons only her heart dared to guess, she looked me up. Our friendship rekindled, and, eventually, we found our guilty way to bed. Elizabeth would be a fine, earnest wife; but I lack the courage either to marry her or to end our affair. A part of me loves her, but not enough to want her as my wife—and I feel like crap because of it. I tell myself I need to go my solitary way, to walk alone, not because of any heroic pretensions, but because I can't allow myself to share my desperate solitude.

Yeah, right.

Three cheers for rationalization.

I banished thoughts of Elizabeth and decided to telephone Larry Norton at the Gazette.

"Norton here."

"Farnigan."

"I dropped by," he said.

"I know. The landlady told me."

"She's a real bitch, Bob."

"You must have caught her without enough muscatel in her. Old Irma is okay enough when she's got a heat on," I said, adding, "but beware when she's got a hangover."

"Pretty bad?"

"When she has a real killer she runs around raising the rent and bitching about the way we abuse her goddamn flats. A real terror in a flannel housecoat."

"Maybe she wants to get laid," Larry suggested. "It's one way to forget a hangover."

"Don't know about that. When she makes it up to my flat, I just give her a glass or two of wine. Doctor Farnigan at her service."

We laughed.

"Look, Bob, you still on the Thanatos thing?"

"More than I want to be," I said.

I brought Larry up to date. He punctuated my narrative with a few "shits," a couple of "goddamns," and even a "fuck." He really was interested in L'Affaire Thanatos.

"Who was the guy in the Mercedes, Bob?"

"Wish I knew, Larry." I lied, not wanting to clue him in on Salomon yet.

There was a moment of silence.

"You did have something for me, didn't you?" I asked. "I'm sure you didn't come by here to see Irma the landlady."

"That's so, Bob." He paused reflectively. "But Irma is an attraction."

"How's that?"

"Ever check out her butt? One bun is higher than the other. Check it out.

"I'll be all eyes." Christ, I thought, Larry must have juiced up somewhere on his way back to the Gazette. When he was in his prime and on a story he never would have bothered about a landlady's displaced bun. "So, what do you have for me?"

"Okay, Bob. I talked to McGrath about Thanatos. I was subtle. You know, asking him if anything ever came of his digging around. He said he was getting bits and pieces, but the editor told him to back off, that there was no news in cults anymore. Anyway, Phil said he was disappointed about dropping the story because he'd come across a pissed off former member of Thanatos who wanted to cry long and loud."

"Who?"

"That's the hell of it, Bob. It's that Richard Kelland—the guy the Mertons talked to you about."

"This is a break, Larry, if I can get him to talk. Does McGrath know where Kelland is?"

"Last known address is the American Hotel on Market near Seventh."

"It's a dump."

"Yeah, Bob, one of your quickie palaces."

"Even I rarely go there, Norton. The American Hotel is the real end of the line."

"Then he's taken quite a fall."

"When you hit the American Hotel you've gone beneath the bottom. No wonder he's pissed at Thanatos."

"Go get him, Bob."

I told Larry I would, then I thanked him for his help and renewed my promise to give the Gazette firsts on any story. In an outburst of honesty we did not go through our usual routine of promising to see each other.

I got out my address book and looked up the number of the wino night manager of the American Hotel. Lyle Benson owed me one for a matter of a dead prostitute, some stolen heroin and a cover-up that had almost gone sour. Lyle was reasonably coherent when I talked with him over the phone, but he was not ecstatic at hearing my voice. He did tell me that Richard

Kelland had a room there, and that Kelland was crazy with anger.

A real detective, I suppose, would have been overjoyed with this much fruitful armchair labor. Me, I was depressed. Why couldn't I find a dead end and be able to write this one off?

Bob Farnigan, Man of Destiny.

No, Bob Farnigan, Man of Weariness. Off to bed. Maybe I would wake up in another universe, my troubles over.

Thanatos disturbed me one last time before I fell into a sweaty slumber with thoughts of the man in the Mercedes.

It was the stuff of nightmares: Harry Salomon in the car, a man of no spiritual aspirations, rather, a man whose universe was that of crime and death.

What was a lord of vice and drugs doing at a fake ashram?

Something to sleep on, I thought, as I lapsed into slumber.

CHAPTER 18

I t was about ten o'clock the next morning when the insistent ring of the telephone, like a bad conscience, jolted me from my uneasy sleep.

"It's Kathy Adams, Mr. Farnigan."

I mumbled, "I've heard of you."

"Shut up, Bob. I have to see you."

"Come this afternoon."

"Now." Her voice was urgent. "I need to see you now."

"What's happened?"

"It's Uncle Skip."

"Dead?"

"No." A hysterical edge came into her voice. "I don't want to talk on the phone. I want to see you now, goddamn it."

"Sure, Kathy. Right away."

"There's a coffee shop next door to my building—"

"At work?" I interrupted.

"Yes, of course. Where else would I be at this hour. Be there in twenty minutes."

"Make it forty-five minutes, Kathy. I've got other business."

"I'm sure you do."

"Really."

"Find a clean shirt," she said as she hung up.

There was no clean shirt found as I hastily dressed, but the one I did wear had no outrageous stains that could not be hidden by my jacket.

Bob Farnigan, Dapper Gent, I thought as I left the flat. I was unreasonably angry with Kathy Adams for wanting her money's worth as I drove downtown. My rage reached cerebral vascular accident level as I attempted to find parking in the crowded maze of downtown San Francisco. As I navigated through my wrath I had misgivings about having had loaded my gun for the first time in years, about actually carrying it. In my current state of mind I might shoot myself, the car, or one of the asshole parking lot attendants who charged seven fifty per half hour for the privilege of dripping oil on their space.

At last, having found a parking space, I legged the three long blocks to the coffee shop. I knew that I was already late and that no excuse would be accepted. True enough. Even a good-looking woman like Kathy Adams was capable of resembling a Gorgon when thoroughly aroused, I would have turned to stone but for the fact that her glare was liquefying me.

"You bastard," she hissed as I sat down.

"I know."

Silent rage and a suggestion of tears.

"I really tried."

"Shut up, Farnigan."

"Yes, ma'am."

She was struggling to regain a hint of civility, and I knew enough to be quiet until she won her battle. So I surveyed the coffee shop, a drab place with ill-matched Formica tables, out-of-balance chairs, and, my God, an ill-tempered middle-aged waitress with hair dyed a nightmare red.

"Want something?"

The hair was blinding.

"Well?"

I had been rendered speechless now by the sight of her long mocha colored fingernails, her guarantee of no deadbeats. Lethal they looked.

"Coffee."

"And?"

"Just coffee."

"Just coffee is two bucks; a buck-thirty-five cents if you order something. Save money and eat—you could use it."

"With this gut, I need it?"

"You eat junk. Eat something good for a change," she said. "You need it."

"Okay. An English muffin and marmalade."

"That it?"

"That's enough."

The flaming angel glared and walked away.

"You infuriate people, Mr. Farnigan."

Kathy had a half smile, a tentative sign of anger deferred but subject to recall. She chain lit a cigarette.

"I wish I didn't anger people, Kathy. I need a break, you know, from my own anger."

A real smile turned quickly serious. She said, "I had a call from Uncle Skip."

"When?"

"This morning, just before I left for work."

"You waited a long time to call me."

"I was told not to."

"By Uncle Skip?"

"In very definite terms." Her lips began to tremble. "He told me that I betrayed him, that I had brought evil into his life."

"Me."

She nodded. For a moment there was a look in her teary

eyes that suggested that she did see me as an agent of darkness. That passed. "He said that you had distressed Doctor Stone. Doctor Stone told Uncle Skip that he had done a grave act of negative karma in showing you Thanatos. When Uncle Skip told me that he also said that he felt betrayed by me."

"You've betrayed no one," I assured her. "Your Uncle's Guide is afraid of losing a fat checkbook."

"I tell myself that, and I suppose it's true; but do I have any right to interfere in what Uncle Skip thinks will save his soul?"

"If you love Uncle Skip, you have a right."

As she nodded, tears ran down her face.

The Red-Haired Demon of San Francisco had managed to deposit my soggy English muffin and filmy coffee by my arm while Kathy had been talking. It seemed a good idea to munch a bit while Kathy restored herself. Maybe some small talk would help.

"Wonderful coffee," I said.

"It's undrinkable."

"True enough, Kathy. But it has potential."

"For what?"

"I could take some home to remove the wax from my kitchen floor."

She laughed more than she should.

"It was a nasty trick," I told her, "to have Uncle Skip call you like that."

"I cried and cried. I was late to work and all I could do was go to the restroom and cry some more."

I held her hand. There were no words to speak. So we sat in a seedy coffee shop, the Henna Harridan giving me "dirty old man" looks, and let the quiet do its work. I am not much on reveries, usually because I begin to feel sorry for myself, resuscitating old disappointments and resentments, but this time I could only think of Kathy. It was a difficult universe, I decided, that would entrust a young woman like Kathy into my care, a cosmos with a macabre sense of humor; but I felt an odd feeling of "rightness," a conviction that helping her was what I should be doing, what I had been preparing for somehow over the years.

Was I frightened by this epiphany?

A dumb question, believe me.

Most men would feel more calm on a suicide mission.

I had faced my own failure and purposelessness with numbness, junk food and alcohol. Happy I wasn't, but I had adjusted. Now this scared girl was forcing me to try to be the man I had never even dreamed of being.

Don't let this new and improved self-image bother you, I told myself, because it too shall pass.

I found all this self-examination unbearable and clumsily scrambled to my feet in a convincing imitation of St. Vitus' dance.

"Let's go."

Kathy looked bewildered, so I repeated myself. "Let's go. Now."

I dropped some money on the table for Medusa who immediately began walking toward the table, no doubt convinced I was going to short her. Bitch.

About forty minutes later Kathy and I were being stared at by Uncle Skip in Fairfax.

"So you brought this person here again."

"Please, Uncle Skip..." she began, but he was having none of it.

"You are interfering in my life, you're endangering my living soul with this godless snooping."

"Look here, Mr. Merton."

"Shut up, Farnigan."

"The hell I will, Merton!"

"I don't know who you are, Farnigan, but you are not welcome here, and neither is my niece as long as she insists on dragging you into my life."

Kathy sort of whimpered at that, looking desperately from Uncle Skip to me.

"Mr. Merton, I don't understand your hostility for us."

"I have no anger toward any living creature," he said with a smile as reassuring as a cobra's. "There is no room in my life for the evils of the world, and that is why I have withdrawn from the world. I do not need intrusions by the unenlightened, the lost."

"Thanks a lot, Mr. Merton."

"Repentance rather than sarcasm would better suit you."

"Sure. Then I could starve on brown rice and make a nice kid like Kathy miserable."

"I love my niece."

"I can tell. All you do is make her cry."

"I love her," he repeated, "but not enough to let her interfere in my life."

In a choked voice Kathy said, "I can't stand this." She turned away from her Uncle Skip and ran back to my car. For a moment I thought I would follow her, but then I looked at Merton. Never had a man looked at me with such hatred. I felt my feet sweating.

"Goddamn your soul, Farnigan," he hissed. "You have corrupted the only person I ever loved."

"Bullshit. Uncle Skip, you reek of bullshit—your own and your two-bit swami's. You're scared of dying. So what do you do? You kill yourself with an idiot diet, you opt for pseudo-mystical brain death, and then you throw away Kathy's love. Don't blame her or me for what you are. You're selfish, stupid and cowardly."

Instead of increasing, the hatred had vanished from

Merton's face during my harangue. What I now saw was an old, frightened man who seemed to be pleading for understanding.

"I realize that you hold me in contempt, and I would have felt that way, too, at one time." He shook his head. "It is true that I fear death, perhaps because I ignored its reality for so long. Like so many others I didn't believe that death applied to me. So when I did become truly aware of the reality of death, it overwhelmed me, and I saw it everywhere, the only reality. Death had transformed everything else into an illusion."

"And you had no faith to fall back on."

"That's what happened."

"I think it happens to all of us. A time comes when we no longer kid ourselves about being immortal. It's no fun, but we can't die prematurely to fear just because we are going to pass away eventually."

"Do you believe in an afterlife, Mr. Farnigan?"

"It's what I was brought up to believe."

"That's no answer."

"Right."

"Well," he insisted, "do you believe?"

"I hope that I can believe."

"You don't seem like a man who runs on hope."

"Not very well."

"Well, I do believe." His smile was triumphant. "I will live on when my body crumbles. A mercy which was wholly undeserved brought me to the man you call a 'two-bit swami.' He accepted my fear, my spiritual barrenness and wasted life without harshness or condemnation and showed me a path for reclaiming my life and my soul."

"If, in return, he could run your life," I added. Anger stirred in Merton again.

"You will not understand what I am trying to tell you."

"There's no problem understanding your words. What I fail

to comprehend is how you can accept the effects of what you believe."

"I accept all, and I reject what I must." He paused. "I should not be talking to you. Doctor Stone has warned me about you."

"Said I was a lost soul, I suppose," I sneered.

"What he said is of no importance to you."

"Try me."

"Try this, then. You are attempting to exploit a childish concern Kathy feels for me and her Aunt for your own ends, probably monetary."

"Like an inheritance."

He laughed. "There is nothing for you to take. That should have been clear to you before. Leave Kathy alone."

"So you can have her soul saved."

"She's probably lost. What I want is no more of you. Doctor Stone has told me that he cannot tolerate outsiders attempting to gain entry to Thanatos." His voice faltered. "Doctor Stone will bar me and my wife from Thanatos if you don't stop your meddling."

"He said that to you?"

"He did."

"So what is he scared of, if I want to know about him and his Thanatos?"

"Doctor Stone wants no one to befoul his work."

"I'm sure it's foul enough."

"Get out of here. Now."

"Gladly."

"Do not come back."

"I won't. I know a lost soul when I see one."

When I got back in the car with Kathy, Uncle Skip was still standing in the doorway. I wondered how I could have gotten myself involved in this tragedy of fear. Kathy turned to me.

"Please drive off."

"Sure."

We had gone about a quarter of a mile down the road before she spoke again.

"When I was with you two back there, I didn't know whether or not I now hated Uncle Skip. I think I hated him for no longer being someone I once loved."

No reply from me.

CHAPTER 19

I dropped Kathy off downtown. She wanted to be alone, to walk about by herself. That was fine by me. There is something about a sufferer, which Kathy was, that made me want to be rid of her. Suffering is unlikable, even if you like the afflicted one.

So it was with a sense of relief that I parked the car in front of my apartment building. I decided to go into my office-garage for a long aimless sitting session, perhaps an hour or two of contemplation of the oil stains on the floor.

When I opened the door, I knew that I should have gone anywhere else, even to confession. Standing by my desk were Charley Cudder and Hal Smith. I wondered if my health insurance was paid up to date.

"This place is a dump, Farnigan," said Hal.

"Call me Bob."

"A real sewer, shithead."

Hal was, as usual, eloquent. He was a short, thin, wiry man whose notion of sartorial elegance included his ever-present teal blue polyester sports coat. Oddly enough, he wore designer shirts and ties that served to intensify his lack of taste. I walked over near the oil slick.

"Nice jacket, Hal," I said. "You trying to be the best dressed hood in town?"

A rumble came from Charley Cudder. "You in need of some pain."

Pain was Charley's business. He was a muscle man with the IQ of a wart. Hal was his keeper. At six-five and three hundred-plus pounds Charley was impressive. Beneath his fat was a lot of hard, mean muscle. It was said that Charley's great love in life was beating people to death. If you survived a Charley Cudder beating you were damned to feel agonizing reminders of it the rest of your shortened life.

"How's Weight Watchers most wanted man?" I asked Charley.

His flat, fat face wrinkled. Another rumble issued from his thin, too small mouth. "Maybe I should feed you your own fat."

"Maybe we should be pals."

"Shit.

"Shut up, you two," said Hal as he leaned against my desk.

"Sure. You talk, Hal."

"Look, Farnigan, we aren't here to mess you up. Nobody told us to do that. We just want to make you understand one little thing."

"I'll try."

"Back off Oscar Merton, his family and that bitch niece of his."

"That it?"

"Simple, isn't it?"

"Not really. I sure want to please you and Charley, but I got to make a living. I'm being paid to keep tabs on Uncle Skip."

"Give the girl her money back, Farnigan. You couldn't earn it anyhow."

My professional pride was hurt.

"I'm not that bad a detective, Hal."

Hal snorted, and Charley looked like he had gas. They thought I was joking.

"I don't understand why I should drop this case."

"Because we're telling you to," said Hal.

"For the sake of your health, asshole," Charley added.

"Who cares about it? Harry Salomon?"

Hal was exasperated. "We do, and that's enough for you. Give back the money to the bitch, or keep it. We don't care. Just lay off. You can always go back to taking nasty pictures in motel rooms."

"Yeah, me and Ansel Adams."

"Who?"

"Never mind."

They were staring at me. The mood was unfriendly. Hal and Charley had no regular employers, they were free agents, like baseball players. But like ball players they didn't come cheap. A visit from Hal and Charley meant I was in over my head. Salomon was using hired muscle to lean on me this time, not Gray Eyes and Smiley, the goons that had roughed me up when I was on Melissa Brinton's trail.

"You aren't stupid, Farnigan," Hal said in his winningest manner. "You've played ball with us before."

"The Knox divorce."

"Right. We told you to lay off Mr. Knox and you did."

"I didn't like that job anyhow." I paused. "Why did you want me to quit the Knox job?"

"Ancient history, Farnigan, but still none of your business. Let us just say that he knew people that wanted their anonymity."

"I said nothing."

"You're a bright boy, Farnigan."

"Thanks."

"So you're off this Merton business."

"No."

"Not smart."

"But I'll think about it."

"Not good enough."

Charley stirred, his fists clenched.

"Okay, I'll quit," I lied.

Hal smiled, but Charley looked disappointed. Hal looked at Charley. "Do you think he means it?"

"I do," I yelled.

"No," said Charley.

For a huge man Charley moves fast. It was like being hit by the 49er front line. He slammed me into the wall and methodically pounded me against it. Charley grabbed me by my jacket and using all of his weight and muscles banged my upper body against a cross beam. I was disoriented, dizzy, filled with jolting pain. I think I was babbling.

"You're hurting the wall," I heard Hal say. Hal's a real wit.

I was just beginning to slide down the wall to the floor after Charley let go of me when Charley's fist slammed into my stomach. It felt as if his fist had ploughed through fat and guts all the way to my spine. I doubled over in agony, nauseated, blind with pain.

"The fucker's puked on my shoes," I heard Charley yell from another universe as I lay in a fetal position on the floor.

Charley had a plan for cleaning his shoes. He began kicking me.

"Not his head," Hal yelled.

Some help. My back and shoulders were being destroyed. The head hardly mattered. Each kick sent a shuddering burst of pain through my body. I felt enveloped in a sea of agony.

"Lay off, Charley." Hal's voice was even more distant, barely cutting through the throbbing in my head. "No more kicks."

"He puked on me."

"Hell, they always do."

"Yeah and they it get worse than he has."

Silence.

"Is he out, Charley?"

"Think so."

"Okay. Let's get out of here."

More silence.

"What are you waiting for, Charley?"

"He puked on me. I don't like it. I want more of him."

"Lay off, I said." Hal was playing boss now. "We weren't even told to pound him, you know."

"So what?"

"If we damage him too much we've got troubles."

"Sure."

"Look, Charley, we get paid for doing what we're told to do."

"Yeah, yeah."

I heard Charley moving away, thankful for no farewell kick. He was muttering.

"We have another call to make," Hal said. "You can do your thing on that one."

"Yeah." Charley sounded like a happy birthday boy.

When I heard the door close behind them I whispered, "Fuck you." I hoped they didn't hear me.

Too late I removed my gun from my shoulder holster and placed it next to me on the floor.

CHAPTER 20

I lay on the floor for a long time, maybe an hour, my sole object of ambition being not to move at all. A true Pollyanna would have been rejoicing that he had not been the recipient of the worst Charley Cudder could achieve. Painful as it was, what Charley had done to me was a warm up for him. I'm fat and out of shape, but I resolved to somehow make Charley Cudder suffer. I also wanted my neighbors to suffer. It seemed to me that someone should have heard the beating of Boris Farnigan, been curious, and offered some sort of assistance. No such luck. The old man who lived in the apartment above my office-garage was deaf, one of those old farts who won't buy a hearing aid so he can have the pleasure of screaming at people to speak up. Mr. Deaf had an excuse, but I was unimpressed by my normally nosy neighbors new found reclusiveness.

So I crawled across the floor, oil spot and all, to my desk and chair. It was decision time: dare I try to crawl into my chair? I really didn't want to elevate my head, to stir up more pain. However, considering my neighbors, if I did nothing I would probably lay here 'til I died and liquefied, like an abandoned cat in a locked cellar. Up I went. Several times. My collisions with the floor when I failed to make it onto the chair were painful beyond belief. Once I made it onto the chair and the throbbing in my head abated, I felt I had made the right decision.

The phone rang. Every nerve rebelled against its shrillness. With as much haste as a man who thinks he's dying can muster, I grabbed the phone.

"Bob?"

It was Kathy Adams.

"I can't talk now."

"Busy."

"Hurt.

"I'll be right there."

"Don't bother unless you've got a new body for me."

"What happened?"

"Your Uncle Skip has some friends who sent a pair of bullies—actually, one bully and his keeper—to persuade me to drop you as a client. They were, as they say, physical. I'm a mess, the office is a mess, and I'm considering going to Lourdes."

"Call the police," she suggested.

"No way. First of all, seven thousand people would swear that Charley and Hal, that's their names, were busy caring for poor little orphans all day today. Secondly, they would visit poor me again, and I don't want to be a guest of honor at a requiem."

"I see." There was a thoughtful silence. "Bob..."

"Yes."

"Are you going to give up?"

"No," I said. "But I'm going to be sneakier."

"Maybe you should quit. I wouldn't blame you. I don't want you to be hurt."

"I am hurt, Kathy. My feelings are also hurt. I'm mad."

"I know."

"I think you do. I appreciate your concern, but I don't want to quit now. I may be a lousy detective, but I have a little pride."

"I don't want you hurt or killed."

"Neither do I. But even second-raters have to have their chance. I need to do this for me. You, too," I added.

Something had been at the back of my aching memory. As I spoke with Kathy, I remembered Richard Kelland. So I gave her a hearty send-off, promising to see a doctor, take good care of myself, brush my teeth and say my prayers.

Since my memory came through, I felt better. No way to explain it, I guess. Maybe my satisfaction in still having a functioning brain stimulated an adrenalin rush. I was sore, but my head was clear, the throbbing gone, and I felt an odd sense of purpose and strength. With a surprising lack of pain I got up from my chair, promised myself to mop the mess tomorrow before it got too ripe, and left the office.

Once in the hallway heading for the back door that lead to the outside stairs up to my apartment, the landlady stuck her head out from her first-floor apartment.

"Pretty rowdy in the garage, Farnigan."

(Would it help my sense of self-esteem to brutalize an old lady?)

"Just my judo lesson, Irma."

"Be more quiet next time."

"Yeah."

She was glaring at my torn, befouled clothes. "You're a mess."

I nodded.

"Drinking again, I bet."

"No. I couldn't stand to look at you with a hangover."

"Go to hell."

She slammed the door.

Up in the apartment I quickly but carefully showered, shaved and got into some nearly presentable clothes. A trip to the refrigerator convinced me that I was not yet able to eat. It also gave me the uneasy feeling that something green and unidentifiable had moved in its dish.

Nonetheless, I was rushing about in my best fat, aching way. Something that Hal had said had me moving fast. He and Charley had another call to make, and it only made sense that it was tied into this Thanatos business. They had warned me off. I guess Kathy Adams was untouchable so far—after all, beating on Kathy might be enough to rouse Uncle Skip from never-never-land. So, I reasoned, the likely candidate for a visit from the Friendship Brothers was Richard Kelland, the impoverished and embittered former devotee of Thanatos. He was a man with a grudge, someone who should not be airing his grievances. I should have talked with Richard Kelland before, I thought reproachfully. Would he talk after a visit from Hal and Charley?

With more luck than I deserved, my punchy mind recalled that he was supposed to be living in a skid row hotel, the American Hotel.

All skid row hotels are the same. Carpeting is dirty and worn to a transparency that exposes the floor beneath, walls are covered with stained and peeling faded wallpaper, and the hallways are dim with the dying light of weak light bulbs suspended from bare wires and smell like urine. Such is the American Hotel, the resting place for the luckless, the defeated, and the castaways, a place for a ruined man like Richard Kelland.

Despite my concern for my car being parked in a tow-away zone (would they take it to a garage or junkyard?), I couldn't avoid somber thoughts in the gloomy lobby. Two straight-back chairs and a lopsided table furnished it; at the other end, a wire cage held enclosed the night clerk. As I approached the cage I smelled the bittersweet odor of muscatel and unfiltered cigarettes.

The wino night clerk woke up to the sound of my hand strumming over the wire cage. He was a stranger to me. Lyle Benson must be sleeping it off somewhere else tonight.

"What do you want?"

"Richard Kelland. He lives here."

His sunken, bloodshot eyes showed both recognition and fear. A bony hand rubbed the white stubble on his face. "Richard Kelland," he repeated.

"Good for you. Your short-term memory is still functional."

"Why should I tell you?"

"Because I've had a bad day and I'm feeling mean."

He looked me over and concluded that even I could make trouble for an old wino.

"Room 211. Same as I told your pals."

"Two men?"

He nodded.

"A mountain and a little shit?"

Another nod.

"When were they here?"

Silence. The wino was thinking. It looked painful and he began to sweat. He was scared.

"I seen nothing. Not even you."

I headed up the dingy stairs. I heard the wino repeat, "Seen nothing."

The room was midway down the hall on the second floor. I knocked, but there was no answer. I knocked louder, but the only response was silence and the opening, furtively, of the door of the next room.

"Something's wrong," said a voice, female, from that open door.

"I know."

"You a cop?"

"No. A friend."

A girl, maybe twenty, stepped into the hall. She had blonde, fresh from the farm good looks. A shy smile revealed two missing lower front teeth.

"Jimmy, my boyfriend, tells me not to talk when he's gone. He's going to get a job in a rock band. Then we can leave here."

"I wish him luck."

"Your friend's in trouble." She nodded towards the door. "There were awful sounds in there."

"What kind? Screaming? Yelling?"

"No, banging, thumps. It felt like the whole place was shaking."

"When?"

"About an hour or so ago. I was scared. I don't think anybody has moved in there since then."

"Yeah."

"Jimmy says don't mess with the people here." She said it as a declaration of faith.

I said, "Jimmy's right."

I told her to stand away from the door. The scared wino would not, I was sure, help me open the door, so sore Farnigan had decided to break it down. Flophouse door are flimsy, the locks and hinges old and rusty, so I figured I could handle it. Even so, please believe me, busting down a door isn't easy—television doesn't tell the truth. For a recently battered man like me even this one was almost too much, but to the sound of splintering wood and the metallic whine of the violated lock, the door burst open.

The light was on inside.

From behind the girl screamed, ran down the hall and rushed down the stairs.

I looked at Richard Kelland. He had his mouth stuffed with a couple pairs of socks, his face was unrecognizable as human: bloody, livid, and puffy. Charley had done his work. One eye stared with the dull certainty of death.

"Holy shit," I said. Then I made the sign of the cross.

CHAPTER 21

I guess the poor kid next door had run out and called the cops, or maybe it was the wino. Who knows? But believe me, I had cops all over me. I didn't even have time for a good snoop around the room. Any search would have been but a nod in the direction of accepted procedure, for Hal and Charley would have left nothing of interest behind. So, anyhow, here were a half dozen cops, a photographer, and a grumpy deputy coroner. As I might have figured, the adrenalin high was gone by now.

Being the imposing figure that I am, the cops told me simply to stay in the hall and not to move, casting baleful looks in my direction occasionally to check on my obedience. This was fine by me. So far I had only identified myself and told them who I thought the corpse was. Hell, even if I had known him intimately I could not have recognized him. Charley Cudder was to a human face what a food processor was to a tomato.

I was exhausted and my hardest task of the day was before me: constructing a believable story that would shelter Kathy Adams and keep me out of jail with my detective license still valid. Right, you're asking why I didn't tell all. Fair enough question. My reasoning told me that if I went the kiss and tell route there would be a lot more bodies, mine prominently among them. Alibis for Hal and Charley were to be assumed for sure. But if I was telling tales their employer, Harry Salomon, would probably want any potential tracks covered up. Fast. That strongly indicated funeral services for Farnigan, Kathy Adams, and even Uncle Skip and Aunt Juliet. Now I think Uncle Skip is a pain in the ass, and his putative Thanatos brainwashing had only accentuated a tendency for being a stuck-up prick, so I wouldn't cry if he went. Who knows, Thanatos would probably do the posthumous roasting, giving Uncle Skip some small return on his investment. But the other lives concerned me, particularly mine.

My creative fiction had begun to come together when the cops decided it was time for chit-chat. What little luck I had been having was holding. The homicide man in charge was Lt. Randall Schmidt. Lt. Schmidt was San Francisco born and raised, a good family man, and a hard-working cop. Around my age, Schmidt was fairly tall, a little overweight, and an obvious friend of the bar stool—his friendly, beefy face had the pink, broken-veined glow of a seasoned drinker. We'd known each other for years, mainly through our mutual friend, Father Daniel Brendan Fahey. Lt. Schmidt and I even played chess from time to time.

"Jeez, what are you doing in this sort of place, Bob?" Lt. Schmidt shook his head. "This guy wasn't one of your adulterous husbands was he?"

"Not him—far as I know."

"So why is he dead?"

"Enemies."

"Don't be evasive, goddamn it."

I feigned outrage.

"His death is a shock to me, Mac. I don't do heavy duty

work. Hell, Mac, you know I don't like trouble. I don't even carry a gun."

"You're still avoiding the question."

"It's so simple, I'm afraid you won't believe me."

"I'll make every effort, Bob." He glared at me. "If I think you're bullshitting me, I'll have your ass."

"I'm going to tell Father Dan about your disgraceful language, you being a paid-up member of the Holy Name Society and all."

"If you do, I tell him about your morals."

I said, "You don't know anything about that."

"But I'm a good, creative liar," he replied.

We laughed uneasily. It was time to try my story out.

"All I can say is that I was a sort of friend. Richard Kelland was a down and outer. You know the type. He had a family, money, good job—the whole thing—but he lost it all. I don't know how. I don't think it was women or booze or gambling. He never said. But he sure nursed a big grievance against somebody. I think somebody did him out of everything."

Schmidt nodded. "So how do you know him?"

"You know me. I attract the unlucky, the guys whose lives haven't worked out. I met him six months or so ago out in Golden Gate Park. I don't think he talked much to anybody, but he felt like spilling that day. He didn't trust anyone, I think, but I caught him when he needed to talk."

"So you became friends."

"No, not friends." I paused in an attitude of reflection. "We just knew each other. I only learned where he lived through accident, a slip of the tongue on his part." I sighed. "So we saw each other six or seven times over a three-four month period. Then...nothing. He was on my mind today. For a few days. Frankly, things have been rough. Little work, less money, lots of bills, and my love life stinks."

Schmidt smiled in spite of himself. Now was the part of the tale that worried me. I had to hope that the wino night clerk was too scramble-brained and scared to mess up my story.

Schmidt prodded me on. "So you came to pay a little social call at this late hour."

"Sure it was late—not that late, though—and my misery needed company. So I drove down here." I started waving my hands. "Oh, dear God! My car's in a tow-away zone. Christ almighty, I hope it isn't towed. Can you help me, Mac?"

"I don't count for shit with the Traffic Bureau, Farnigan." The surname showed his impatience. "Tell me about tonight."

"All right. I came by here, saw the wino at the desk, and asked for Richard Kelland. Funny thing, he told me that two other guys had come to see Kelland and I almost left. But I decided what the hell. When I got up here, I knocked a few times. No answer. Then the little girl—young woman—in the next room came out. Have you talked to her?"

Schmidt nodded.

I continued. "She said it sounded like there had been a beef in Kelland' room. Lots of noise. Said it had scared her. So I busted the door."

"Just like that," Lt. McGuire was sarcastic.

"Sure."

"Ever hear of keys?"

"Yeah. I'd also seen the shit-faced wino. Hell, he was almost passed out when I got here. Anyhow, I felt something. Something told me there was big trouble. That's how it was."

Schmidt looked at me intently, as if trying to decide. At last he spoke.

"I'll buy your story. It's weak enough to be the truth." He laughed humorously. "I never believe anybody anymore. Never believe you guys with a license in particular. You're almost as bad as lawyers."

I could tell that Schmidt wasn't satisfied, but I knew he had nothing to challenge me with. The girl next door would corroborate me and the wino would be lost in his own fog—if my luck held. It also helped that I left my gun back at the office. Having it with me would have made my social call story weaker than it was.

Schmidt lost interest in me.

"You're going to have to make a statement down on Bryant Street."

"Sure."

"We'll drive you down, take your statement, and drive you back here since you're a friend." He paused and added with Irish malice, "Maybe your car will still be here."

I didn't say what I wanted to say.

It was after midnight when I got back home. Schmidt had been rather sullen while taking my statement but he had made no trouble for me. For my part, I told the story again as I had told it in the hallway, resisting any temptation to polish my creative effort. When it was given to me to read I felt like William Shakespeare—or at least Mickey Spillane. I signed the statement, made the standard promises about being available, and got my ride back to the tow-away zone. I had to listen to some abuse about the car, but at least it was there, although what would be a costly citation had been affixed. But not to complain.

I went home.

I was exhausted as I sat on my sofa. Bones screamed, my brain was numb. I felt a weariness that suggested death itself. As I began to stretch out to sleep, not wanting to make the impossible journey to my bed, the goddamn phone rang, the first of two calls.

It was Hal.

"You don't listen, do you?" he said. "We gave you a friendly warning today. I even kept Charley from killing you after you puked on him. I wish I hadn't done that now."

I yelled at the mouthpiece. "You bastards! You fucking killers!"

"Shut up, Farnigan." The voice was icy. "You're going to die. You'll die slower than Kelland. Get me? You want to live, Farnigan, you back off, you get lost, you leave town. No more warnings."

The phone went dead.

CHAPTER 22

Believe me, I am not a brave man. I was scared. If Charley had not already made me lose my internal contents, I think I would have done so then. That's how scared I was after the call. My heart was racing, I was short of breath. Eventually, though, I calmed down, the aching, total weariness returned, and, yes, the phone rang again.

It was Kathy Adams, almost as scared as I was. The hysteria in her voice made my weariness but a memory. "Bob! It's just too horrible," she cried.

"For Christ's sake, what's happened?"

She was sobbing.

"I can't ... I can't stand it. It's so horrible."

"Kathy, please tell me what happened. Has someone hurt you?"

"Bob, they..." She could only cry. "Someone's been here."

"You're home, aren't you?"

"Yes."

"I'll be right there."

She said, "I don't know if..."

"I'm on my way. You'll be all right 'til I get there, won't you?"

"Yes," she said. "Hurry."

It didn't take any great intellect to know that Kathy had been leaned on by the same crowd that was making my life miserable.

I hurried to my battered car and it set a new record for successive starts in one day. My own sense of urgency seemed to have an effect on the car. I'm talking speed—at least for my heap. Lapsing into anthropomorphic discourse, I lavishly praised my green oil burner.

Yet my thoughts were on Kathy, Richard Kelland, Hal and Charley, me and Harry Salomon. When I had visited the good Dr. Stone at Thanatos and saw Harry Salomon in the Mercedes, I didn't want to believe Salomon was involved in Thanatos. Vice, drugs, extortion and every other loathsome subhuman enterprise were Salomon's business. He was a man feared for his gleeful ruthlessness, and now I know he had some sort of interest in Thanatos, and that interest had grown to include Kathy Adams and me. We were no longer safe. From all that I knew of Harry Salomon, he wasn't trying to warn us off, but was playing cat and mouse, sadistically biding time until his hired claws tore us apart.

With those happy thoughts driving me towards the near side of panic I found myself knocking on Kathy's apartment door about twenty minutes after her call.

A quavering voice said, "Who is it?"

"Farnigan."

After much fumbling with an assortment of locks the door opened and I looked into Kathy's teary, desperate face. She pointed in the direction of her kitchen. "In there," she said.

The apartment was a mess, I noticed as I walked toward the kitchen. End tables and chairs had been overturned, books scattered from their shelves, and a large picture lay shattered against the far wall. Salomon's boys had done a real professional job. Again, no doubt, neighbors had listened with willful ignorance.

In the kitchen, dangling from a rope attached to a light fixture, was Kathy's Siamese cat. Beneath it, on the floor, were its guts; the cat had been butterflied.

From behind me Kathy said, "I loved that cat."

I turned, silently took her hand, and led her to her sofa.

"Sit here, Kathy. I'll take care of it."

She nodded.

"Do you have any brandy?"

Another nod, she pointed toward the kitchen.

I found the brandy with no difficulty and brought her a drink. She attempted a smile when she noticed that I served the brandy in a water glass. Believe me, I'm all class.

I returned to the kitchen after saying some of those weak consoling words that do neither good nor harm. Fighting down a growing nausea, I untied the rope from the light fixture and slid the Siamese into a plastic trash bag. Using newspapers and paper towels I cleaned up the bloody, offal-laden floor. I hoped that Kathy was more practical than sentimental as I deposited my grisly mop up in the old-fashioned garbage chute to the basement.

It seemed that I spent an eternity of fastidiousness washing my hands and arms over and over again in the kitchen. Satisfied that I was physically, if not psychically, clean, I found a coke in the refrigerator and returned to the living room to sit next to Kathy in silence.

"Did you see anyone?"

She shook her head.

I waited until, at last, she spoke.

"Hold me."

I took her glass from her hand and placed it next to my coke. I held her, listening to our scared breathing.

"I'll never go in there again," she said. Her head made a motion in the direction of the kitchen.

"It's all right now," I said lamely.

"Except that I'll always see my poor little Winston." She began to cry again.

I listened to Kathy sob and hated Hal and Charley and Harry Salomon. At that moment, holding this lovely, crying woman, I came near to renouncing God, to believing that the Creator of such a world had to be evil Himself—the dark night of the soul.

"You should try to sleep," I said.

"I know."

"I'll stay here on the sofa and sleep. For what I'm worth, I will guard you."

She looked at me, a faint smile on her pale lips. "I'll try to sleep, Bob. Thanks."

"Go get ready for bed."

She got up silently from the sofa and disappeared into her bedroom. As I listened to the random mysterious sounds of a woman preparing for sleep, weariness reasserted itself. With no little effort I rose and turned off the lights in the living room, more exhausted than ever when I returned to the sofa. I closed my eyes for a few moments but opened them again as I became aware of Kathy's presence.

Kathy stood in the bedroom looking young and fragile. She was wearing a short, transparent nightshirt that hid no anatomy. My conscience howled at me for taking any erotic notice of Kathy Adams. In the doorway she stood; she seemed incapable of movement or speech. I walked over to her.

"Please go to bed, Kathy," I said. "We both need to rest. We have too much to do, to decide on. We'll need our rest for tomorrow."

I led her to her bed. She did not want to get under the covers, instead she lay on top of the bedspread. I sat on the bed holding her hand in silence. When she spoke her voice seemed distant.

"They hurt you too, didn't they?" she asked.

"Yes. They did."

"Tell me about it."

"No."

"Bob, I want to hear." An odd laugh that was nearly a sob startled me. "It will help to know."

I briefly recounted to her my visit from Hal and Charley, my visit to the American Hotel, Richard Kelland, and hinted at my darker conclusions. She had to be told that Harry Salomon had declared war on us. God knows, I tried to spare her all the horror I could, but I knew that she would see through any dishonesty. When I finished speaking she was crying again.

"Hold me, Bob," she said.

I stretched out next to her and held her again in my arms. A sense of helplessness filled me as I held her, the terrible knowledge that I could not take her pain and sorrow from her. Best I could do was to hold her tightly, occasionally run a free hand through her lovely hair, and whisper again words of solace.

Her crying had stopped several minutes ago and I now felt her stirring in my arms. Soon my head was on her shoulder and her hands were caressing my head. She kept whispering, "Poor, dear Bob."

I don't remember who gave the other the first, tentative kiss, but we were soon kissing with the need to assert passion over pain and hurt. My hands touched her small, firm breasts and then wandered beneath her nightgown.

And so we made love, the ancient love that desperate men

and women have made throughout time to shut out the world's malice. We were every man and woman who had ever loved life more than death.

Our lovemaking was silent and strong, and when done we each fell into a deep dreamless sleep as we still held each other.

CHAPTER 23

It was a little past noon when I woke up in Kathy's bed. I heard sounds from the kitchen and admired her strength. It takes a special courage to face the memory of insane cruelty. And, yes, believe me, my over-refined Catholic conscience began to go into overdrive about last night's lovemaking. Part of me knew that I would lack any conviction in saying it was sinful, but another part had never outgrown the rigid Catholic rules I'd grown up with. I would have to tell Father Daniel Brendan Fahey that my confession was good form, not bad conscience.

My body, thanks to Charley Cudder, was sorer than my conscience, but I lay in bed feeling strong and curiously hopeful. No, I thought, I can't believe in sin, not this time.

Kathy came in with a cup of coffee and a promise of breakfast. I sat up in bed and eagerly drank the coffee from the cup she handed me. I mumbled a sleepy thank you and let the French roast coffee do its work. Farnigan was resurrecting.

Returned to life, my first caffeine fix received, I looked at Kathy. She was wearing faded blue jeans, a tee-shirt that proclaimed her love for the San Francisco Opera, and an awkward, shy look that I understood. Her thoughts were on last night as she watched the middle-aged, overweight Farnigan drink his coffee. I put the coffee on the nightstand.

I said, "About last night."

"Yes."

"You want to talk about it?"

"Yes. I do."

She sat down on the bed, neither too close nor too far from me. "I know we're not lovers," I began, perhaps a mite wistfully. "God knows any man would want to be your man, even Bob Farnigan."

"Don't trash yourself, Bob," she said sharply.

"I won't. I just want you to know that I expect no love affair with you. I'm not going to presume a relationship. Though we sure are good friends now."

She laughed with me and repeated, "We are good friends now."

"And last night was last night," I added.

Kathy stood up and then leaned over me to give me a quick kiss and her last word on the subject. "I'll always love you at least platonically, Bob."

"Me, too," I said.

With Kathy gone to finish preparing a promised breakfast, I began reassembling myself. As I showered I once again proved that a shower stall's acoustic can transform a whiskey baritone into a Wagnerian heldentenor. I took this heroism of mine over to the wash basin and mirror and subjected it to the ultimate trial: shaving with hand-soap and a ladies razor. Back in the bedroom, bloodied and less heroic, I untangled my clothes from the heap next to the bed. Wrinkled and bloodied but clean was Farnigan.

Kathy had done a good job of cleaning up her living room,

only a critical eye could tell that the Huns had marched through the day before. Breakfast—eggs, bacon, toast and coffee—was simple and plentiful. We ate in silence except for the occasional words of request and thanks. I almost managed to forget that I was scared witless.

Well fed, we moved to the sofa. Perhaps to keep me from talking about our troubles Kathy indulged herself in a little sauciness.

"I don't know about you," she said archly, "but I'm always hungry the next morning."

"Many are the hungers," I intoned. "Blessed are they who have their cake and eat it too."

"You're a clown."

We laughed and fell into a prolonged, amused silence. I broke the mood.

"Much as I don't regret it, Kathy, we were foolish to stay here last night. Harry Salomon's got us on his shit list, which means that our chances for long-term survival are pretty dim. He has us where he wants us. My nosing around Thanatos has made him uncomfortable, but I don't have anything on him. Hell, I don't even know why he's interested in us. There's no way to prove a damn thing against him or Hal or Charley or the goon's who came here last night."

"It wasn't your friendly visitors?" she asked.

"No. I don't think so. Salomon would only send Hal and Charley if he had wanted you maimed or worse."

"I see."

"Good." I continued. "Anyhow, if we went to the police all we would get would be sympathy. The cops would probably believe us, but they would tell us they had no evidence, no proof. Maybe, but just maybe, if they were already in a snit at Salomon they might pester him, but not much. Harry Salomon employs enough lawyers to staff a law school. His shysters would eat the cops alive for their cruel harassment of a pillar of the community."

"So we're out in the cold."

"Without an igloo."

She was angry. "So what the hell can we do! You know everything we can't do, Bob. What can we do—that's what I want to know. Do we sit here and wait for Harry Salomon to disembowel us?"

"We lay low. That's what we do."

"You mean we hide."

"We hide."

She was quiet as she thought a moment. "I don't want to hide, Bob."

"I don't like it either. But if we stay in sight or, worse, go to the cops we're all dead—you, me and Uncle Skip and Aunt Juliet. As I see it, Harry Salomon wants peace of mind. I'm hoping that if we disappear for a while, Harry's nerves will calm down, that a happy Harry will forget about us."

"That means we do nothing for Uncle Skip."

"Kathy, Uncle Skip is a lost cause. He's a willing victim who wants no help."

"But we can't abandon him and Aunt Juliet."

"Back in my unenlightened youth we used to say that someone was free, white, and twenty-one. That meant, among other things, that people made their own choices. Your Aunt and Uncle have made a bad choice but it's their choice. They're stuck, we're stuck."

"You don't care about them," she accused me.

"I do, Kathy. But, again, we're powerless unless they want our help."

"We have to do something."

"We have to stay alive to be good for anybody."

I thought for a while. An idea came to me, but I didn't like it.

The idea had nothing to go for it. Quixotic, dangerous, and futile—a typical Farnigan brainstorm. I would have despised myself for it if Kathy hadn't decided to announce the same plan to me.

"Bob, let's take a last chance."

"And..."

"We'll try to reason with my Aunt and Uncle one last time. If I try to tell them what's happened maybe they'll want to leave Thanatos and Doctor Stone."

I was skeptical. "Sure they will."

"They really care about me. I know it would shock them if they knew what I have been through, if they knew about poor Mr. Kelland, about you,"

"It might work but it's a slim hope. We have to overcome their faith and fear too. Even people who deprogram cult victims don't always have success."

She was firm.

"They deserve a last chance,"

I told her that a direct approach to them was foolish.

We would have to get them to come to us, assuming they had any freedom of movement. Her Aunt and Uncle could not come to her apartment or to my office for obvious reasons. We would need a safe, public meeting place. Kathy remembered a favorite of theirs, the M. H. de Young Museum in Golden Gate Park. That sounded good.

I said, "First of all, Kathy, we go into hiding, in separate places. I have a friend you can stay with." "Who?"

"Elizabeth Casey." I felt embarrassed suddenly. "Elizabeth and I used to be an item. Now we're just friends who probably should have gotten married, but didn't. She used to be a nun so she knows all about taking care of the homeless. You'll like her."

"I don't know, Bob."

"Look. There won't be any jealous woman problem. Like I

say, Elizabeth and I are just friends now. Maybe she still has some faint hopes about marriage. She probably does. But we owe no explanations to each other. Anyhow, you'll just be a lady client in trouble."

"Okay, Bob, if you think it best."

I hope I didn't show my relief.

"After I drop you off at Elizabeth's—she'll be home, school teachers in summer always are—I go back to my office for my gun, fresh clothes, and some other stuff."

"I see."

"When I'm through there, I'll go to my friend Fred's apartment. That's where I plan to lay low."

"What about our plan?"

"I'll contact you tonight and come over to Elizabeth's to figure out how to try to arrange our meeting—your meeting—with Uncle Skip and Aunt Juliet. If we get the meeting, all hell will break loose."

"I know," she said glumly.

"If you convince them to leave, all of you will have to get out of town. I'm talking about real hiding. In the mountains. In sunny old Mexico. Maybe in beautiful Biloxi, Mississippi."

She laughed.

"If you fail, you'll have to leave town anyhow."

"What about you?"

"I have no urge to travel. I'll stay with Fred—if he'll have me. At least for a while."

It was almost three in the afternoon and a lot had to be done. Kathy packed some clothes, make-up, and other stuff in admirable haste. I told her that we should stop at her bank for her to get enough money to finance a sudden trip. She agreed to that and to my using her credit card to rent a car for me, an inconspicuous one to replace temporarily my moving eyesore.

Just as we were leaving the telephone rang.

I answered.

It was Hal. Somehow he knew that I had answered. "First, you die Farnigan," he said. "If that doesn't wise your little bitch up, she dies."

The phone went dead.

I told Kathy it was a wrong number.

CHAPTER 24

Maybe all the world loves lovers and people in flight. Ever try to park in San Francisco? Explaining Einstein to a rock is easier, believe me. But not today. I only had to double park while Kathy ran into her bank. We abandoned my car in a tow-away zone while we went to rent another car for me. If what little that was still valuable wasn't stripped from it before being towed, I figured the impounding would at least keep the car safe until I could bail it out. The snotty clerk at the car rental agency kept looking at me as if I were Kathy's derelict father freshly bailed out of the drunk tank. There is a style sales or service people love to affect when dealing with those they consider shabby, an exaggerated politeness and solicitude that makes me want to crush their skulls.

In the rented Toyota I drove a crazy route to Elizabeth's house. It took me almost an hour and a half to get there, a ridiculous amount of time. But I had to be sure I was not being followed. My route eventually confused me and I got lost in a part of the city I was unfamiliar with. Humiliation aside, I was satisfied with myself when we arrived.

Elizabeth lives in the Sunset district of San Francisco near

Forty-first Avenue and Taraval. Her house was one of those stucco horrors that abound, built wall-to-wall, in the interminable district. As usual for the misnamed Sunset, it was damp and foggy. While we approached her house I fought back the fear that she would not be home. It spoke much of my relationship with Elizabeth that I had taken her being home for granted. In a way, I see Elizabeth as always waiting for me. It is the sorrow of her life that she does wait for me.

After parking, Kathy and I walked up the short way to the door. I could sense Kathy's nervousness. My own nervous system howled in anticipated anguish as Elizabeth was eternally slow in responding to the ringing doorbell.

At last the door opened.

"Hello, Bob," said Elizabeth, her usual smile full of welcome.

"Hi."

She glanced at Kathy. "Who's your friend?"

"A client. Kathy Adams. We're in trouble."

With no nonsense we were hustled into the house. I immediately relaxed as I always do, in the simple comfort of Elizabeth Casey's home. Like herself, Elizabeth's home combines efficiency and warmth, that is, there is no clutter to intrude on the quiet comfort offered. When I need to retreat from chaos, Elizabeth's is the place to be. As she seated us with a smile and rushed off to begin making tea, I began to hate myself for her. She loved me and I loved her, but I had always refused to give up my aimless freedom. I think the reason why we stopped sleeping together was not only Catholic guilt but because of our own sense of incompleteness: we needed the ring and priest to be true lovers. As Elizabeth was now approaching the end of her child-bearing years I wondered if she harbored a secret hatred for me.

"Now tell me your trouble," she said returning from the kitchen. "Tea will be ready soon."

"Sit down, Elizabeth."

"Oh, no. The pot's going to whistle in just a few minutes."

I briefly told her all, interrupted only by the pouring of the strong, black tea. As I spoke part of me was distracted by her special beauty. Elizabeth has a soft, red-haired beauty highlighted by dark eyes that can be filled with poetry or laughter. A bit overweight but still shapely, her body offered warmth and a solid strength. Though calm, worry and fear showed occasionally in her eyes. When I paused, she spoke with purpose, looking at Kathy.

"Of course Bob and you have to try to rescue those poor people. They can't be abandoned to an evil that will kill them body and soul. You're very brave, Kathy." She turned her gaze from Kathy to me. "And Bob, I'm glad you're helping."

"It's my job."

"No, Bob, if it was just a job you wouldn't be this involved. You believe in what you're doing."

"For a change."

"That's what's good for you."

I changed the subject. "So Kathy can stay here?"

"As long as she needs to. Her Aunt and Uncle are welcome too."

"Thank you, Elizabeth," said Kathy, full of relief and gratitude. "I'm a stranger to you. Your kindness is too much."

Kathy had fallen under the spell of Elizabeth's goodness.

"Don't embarrass me, Kathy," said Elizabeth. "I won't lie and say I'd get mixed up in this for just anyone, but I like you, even though I don't know you, and I can tell that Bob likes you. Bob's opinion means a lot to me."

Part of me curled up and died. For a brief moment the urge

to ask Elizabeth to marry me overwhelmed me. The guilt of
Farnigan was at a new summit, or depth, if you please.

Kathy and Elizabeth looked wordlessly at each other.

Feminine communication was going on. It was time to
retreat.

"I have to go. I want to get my gun from the office before
dark."

We all stood. Both women urged me to be careful. I wanted
to remind them of my commitment to craven cautiousness, but I
was stopped by their looks of concern and, God save me, admi-
ration. Their hero was going to slink back to his office, and, with
luck, not shoot himself loading his gun. I didn't know whether to
laugh or cry for them or me.

Kathy stayed in the house while Elizabeth walked with me
to the Toyota. She kissed me and told me she loved me.

I drove away with tears in my eyes.

It was nearly six o'clock when I parked the Toyota three or
four doors up from my garage. As I walked back to the entrance
to my building I noticed that the normal summer late afternoon
mist had yet to reach my neighborhood.

In the hallway of my apartment building a feeling of unease
began to nag me. I was suddenly sweating, my heart racing. I
tiptoed down the hall to the side door to the garage. In true
detective fashion, using the technique acquired from years of
skulking around motel room doors, I bent over and peered
through the keyhole. A true peeper am I. Inside I could see Bad
Trip Leo. He was sitting in my swivel chair, his hand laying on
the desk next to his .357 Magnum.

No one knows Bad Trip Leo's last name. His parents
wouldn't admit their crime. Bad Trip is a hit man, heartless and
vicious. A relic of the Haight-Ashbury, Leo had gotten his nick-
name during some drug wars when small-time pushers used Leo
to knock off rivals, deadbeats and burn artists. A born sadist, Leo

had used a knife in those days to kill his victims slowly. A visit from Leo was the ultimate "bad trip." He graduated to the big-time professional killer game in the late nineties when he traded in his knife for a gun. Bad Trip Leo was regarded in the underworld as cold, cruel, crazy and efficient.

So, a contract was out on me, as Hal had promised. The idea of being a used car salesman in Davenport, Iowa didn't seem like a bad idea right now.

I watched Bad Trip. Fear and fascination had paralyzed me. Bent over the keyhole I was staring at my own death. Bad Trip must have sensed me, smelled my fear-stenched sweat. He began to stir, alert and tense. His hand closed around the gun's handle.

Panic filled me as I stood straight up, desperately looking up and down the hall for a place to hide. Good old drunken Irma. Seven feet up the other side of the hallway I could see her door ajar. She never missed a thing in her building.

My speed must have surprised Irma. Before she could react, I had rushed into her apartment. With an unnatural grace I managed to grab her with one arm and cover her mouth with my free hand. Stretching my left leg behind me I managed to kick the door shut. Irma was limp.

She looked at me with disbelieving terror. I had never seen her wine dimmed eyes clear before.

"Someone is in my office," I whispered hoarsely. "He wants to kill me. Do you understand?"

I saw no comprehension in her eyes.

"A man with a gun wants to kill me. I saw him through the key hole. I saw his gun. We must be very quiet. He'll kill us both if he finds us. Nod if you understand."

She nodded.

"I'll let you go if you promise to be quiet. Not a word. Understand?"

Another nod.

"When I let you go I want you to sit down. Over there." I jerked my head. "Over there by your front window."

Again she nodded. I could see that Irma believed me. That figured. Surely she had seen Bad Trip go into my makeshift office. Irma was too good at snooping to miss him.

I let go and she rushed to the window and sat down. Irma glared at me with fear and hatred.

Outside, in the hallway, were the sounds of Bad Trip in motion. He seemed to be pacing back and forth as if unable to make a decision. I glanced at Irma to make sure she was silent and in place. Satisfied, I turned to peer out into the hallway through the inset one-way peephole in the door.

Bad Trip walked past in the direction of the stairway to the upper floor apartments. He would have no idea that to reach my place, he had to take the outside back stairs. Few people, in fact, realized that.

From the silence outside I could tell that he was standing at the foot of the stairs wondering if I had bypassed my office to go up to an apartment. Perhaps the noises he heard from the hallway had been me en route upstairs. I agonized as he decided. At last I heard the sound of his footsteps as he began ascending the stairs.

Eons passed and galaxies were created and destroyed as I listened until I could no longer hear him climbing stairs.

I turned to Irma and said, "I'm leaving. Stay quiet and you'll be safe."

She said nothing.

I slowly opened the door and slowly crept out into the hallway.

As I carefully shut Irma's door I heard her mutter, "Farnigan. You're an asshole."

With as much silence as my fat body could muster I rushed

into my office. Bad Trip Leo had conveniently left the door open. I tried to pull open the desk drawer that contained my gun. The drawer was stuck. It could not be helped, noise and all, I began wrestling with the drawer. Each second I grew more desperate and convinced that I was making more racket than a wrecking company. The drawer at last gave in to me and slid open. I grabbed my gun and began loading it with bullets from the box of shells in the drawer.

I was standing now with a loaded gun in my hand as I heard the sound of Bad Trip racing down the stairs. Bad Trip Leo would be in the hallway in a moment. If I tried to leave by the hall door I would die. Without thought I raced to the garage door, almost slipping on the oil slick, and lifted the huge door. With a grinding groan the door slid upward far enough for me to duck under it. I was on the sidewalk.

I ran. By now Bad Trip had to be in the garage.

I ran blindly, with no thought, pushed by the lust to survive. In my panic I didn't recognize my rented Toyota and ran past it. When I realized my mistake I was too far beyond the car to return.

It is a conviction of mine, no matter how implausible, that I felt the bullet from Bad Trip's .357 Magnum rocket past my head before I heard the sound of its terrible roar. At least I knew where Bad Trip was. Behind me.

I dropped to the sidewalk and rolled into the street between two parked cars. The rear window of the car behind me exploded as Bad Trip fired again.

On my knees I peered over the trunk of the car. Bad Trip was coming at a dead run. Skinny and pale of face, with no eyebrows and his long hair blowing behind him, Bad Trip looked like a macabre updating of one of the Four Horsemen.

With mindless desperation I stood and fired my gun at him. Red blossomed from Bad Trip's chest and his legs went into a spastic imitation of running. I could see dull puzzlement on his face as he began to fall. The gun must have had a hair trigger because as Bad Trip fell, already dead, the gun fired again and again into the sidewalk.

I stepped onto the sidewalk. Bad Trip had fallen about fifteen feet away. He lay face down, a lake of blood forming around him on the bullet scarred concrete. I stood, arms limp, motionless as a disinterested observer. Windows and doors began opening from the buildings along the street, I heard loud, panicky voices shouting in a babble of shock and excitement. A few brave souls were tentatively walking down the street towards me.

The realization that I had just killed a man became my only reality. I felt no shock, no guilt, no remorse. Never was the thought of prayer for the dead further from my heart. I felt good.

But I did not linger in my joy in death. Aware that a crowd would soon form and that the police were only moments away, I did the only reasonable thing I could think of. I ran.

There were shouts behind me. I stopped, turned, and made a menacing gesture with my gun. It filled my newfound tough guy image with delight when I saw how fast the street emptied. Believe me, I was lucky that there was no local gun nut to come out to play High Noon.

I was running again. When I reached a narrow side street I turned down it until I came to an alley. Neither my lungs nor my heart had any more tolerance for these extraordinary exertions. I began to wonder if cardio-pulmonary arrest would do what the late Bad Trip Leo had failed at. The wheezing and coughing along with the madly thumping heart indicated that it was going to be close. Nausea and waves of faintness engulfed me as I staggered down the alley. In the distance I heard the keening of police sirens. I needed a place to rest, to hide, to think.

My daze gave way to reality when I stumbled with a wrenching jolt into the side of a debris box. The heavy metal container was positioned at the rear of a large apartment building for the tenants to use as a giant, collective garbage can. It had two heavy steel lids, one open, the other closed. When I peered over the edge of the debris box into the open area, I could see that it was better than half filled.

The sirens' wail was getting closer. Glancing about I failed to see anyone in the alley or peering from a rear window. With great difficulty I pulled myself up the side of the debris box and fell head first into it. I remembered that my mother had always warned me in a voice of dire prophecy that my wicked ways would lead me to a life in the gutter. I wondered if this was close enough for her.

CHAPTER 25

L ife in a debris box (or is dumpster the proper name?) is not
as bad as you might think. I had worked my way to the
side of the box that was covered by the heavy lid. A little pulling
and rearranging had made for me a reasonably comfortable
corner. I had gathered some newspapers near me to cover
myself with in case anyone decided to check out the box. It was
hot and odorous inside. Sharp smells of decaying food and
disposable diapers penetrated to nasal passages hitherto unused.
But you can get used to anything. Believe me, after a half hour
or so I was unaware of the stench.

The other end of the debris box, the open side, was falling
into increasing darkness as the sun began its plunge into the
Pacific. It would be night in another hour or so. From time to
time I became aware of the movement of people and cars in the
alley. I guess the police must have gone by at one time or
another, but no one paid any attention to my hiding place.
Believe me, I was most grateful that so far this hadn't been take-
out-the-garbage night for anybody.

I must have dozed off. God knows I was exhausted enough
to sleep anywhere. It was totally dark inside the box when I

awoke. Either it was night or the lid on the other side had been closed. I crawled across the bags of garbage, some broken open, to the other side and saw a few stars flickering through the light evening fog as I looked up. As quietly as I could I climbed out, scraping my knees and shins in my exit as I had on my entrance. My identity seemed to be defined only by my aches and my weariness.

It took me a few minutes to orient myself as I stood next to my malodorous refuge. I had run farther than I had thought possible. There is no underestimating the power of panic. It would be foolish to attempt to go back for the rented Toyota, so I would have to walk—if I could persuade my angry body. I decided to try to make it to Fred's apartment. A look at my watch informed me that my nap had lasted over two hours. It was nearly ten o'clock.

I stayed next to buildings, doing my best to avoid light from streetlamps, as I headed for Fred's. It took the last reserve of nerve to not run while on the exposed street, and it was with relief that I left the street to turn into the alley that ran behind Fred's apartment building. Dim memory assured me that there was a rear entrance to his building. And so there was. It was unlocked, a tribute to premises security; but I was loath to complain.

My lungs were again protesting after I climbed the flights of stairs to Fred's apartment. Visions of cardiac arrest haunted me as I knocked on the door.

The door opened and Fred said, "Ah, my friend the desperado!"

He pulled me inside and shut the door. There was a deeply offended look on Fred's face. "You're a pungent desperado, too. How you do stink."

I started to say something, but Fred interrupted. "It's bath time for Farnigan. You can explain your stench later." He laughed. "I have nothing against harboring fugitives, but don't stink me out."

He began pushing me toward his bathroom.

"You are okay?" he asked.

"Yes. Just tired."

"And too, too dirty."

I stood by the bathtub and Fred began running the water. "Don't spare yourself the soap. It's cheap."

"I won't."

"Good boy, Farnigan. When you take off your clothes, toss them out the door." He made an elaborate gesture of holding his nose. "Thank God I have a washer and dryer."

He left, closing the door behind him. I slowly undressed. Stiff weariness made every motion an exercise in misery. I slid into the bathtub, my clothes in a heap outside the bathroom door, and soaked up the warmth of the water.

Fred called from the living room. "After the clothes are in the washer I'll prepare you a feast, Mr. Dillinger." He added, "I'm wearing gloves to carry your clothes, by the way." He probably was.

When I emerged from the bathroom dressed in a bathrobe of Fred's that scarcely covered anything, I could smell lamb chops frying. Fred called from the kitchen to tell me that dinner was all but ready and that I was to sit myself at the table. Fred continued his cheerful chatter in the kitchen.

"You can tell me all about your trigger-happy day while we eat." He laughed and added, "And tell me where you were wallowing before you got here."

"Mind how you talk to me, Fred," I growled in reply. "I still have the gun."

"Not anymore."

"What?"

"I've got your coat—and the gun's in its pocket."

"So I'm at your mercy."

"Lucky for you. I'm going to feed you."

Fred brought lamb chops, rice and a bottle of white wine to the table. He drank some wine to keep up strength, or so he claimed, while I attacked the chops. He rarely interrupted as I ate and brought him up to date on what he insisted on calling "the Thanatos Caper." When I concluded both dinner and story (good timing) Fred's comment was that he was sure Wyatt Earp never ended up in a garbage can.

"But given all you've been through, Farnigan, I'm going to be a true martyr," he announced. "You can sleep in my bed and I'll sleep on the sofa."

"Thanks."

"You could have insisted on me staying in my own bed," he muttered.

"But I won't. I'm too tired. I have too much to think about and do tomorrow. Anyway, Fred, I've earned a good night's sleep."

I stood up.

"Scarcely a heroic body," said Fred.

"Go to hell."

"If I'd only taken a look before I fed you, it would have been cottage cheese and crackers."

I entered the bedroom while Fred was critiquing my physique, and discarded the bathrobe.

"Jabber all you want to. I'm going to bed," I said as I got into bed.

Fred said, "Sweet dreams, Mr. Spade."

It was after one o'clock in the afternoon when I awoke. Sleep never really restores you if you have pushed yourself beyond your capability, an edge of exhaustion seems to stay with you forever. So, though rested, I was aware of a new permanent weariness. Fred had put my cleaned clothes on a chair next to the bed. I dressed quickly and went into the living room.

Fred was in his favorite chair, reading and drinking a glass of wine.

"The Return of the Falcon."

"No, just me."

"Life disappoints us all." He waved in the direction of the kitchen. "Get yourself some coffee. I wait on fugitives only at night."

When I returned with my coffee and sat down on the sofa I noticed a pile of newspapers on the floor. Fred observed my glance.

"You're quite the celebrity, Mr. Farnigan. They're even talking about you on the radio."

"And..."

"You have their sympathy. Witnesses have convinced them it appears to be a matter of self-defense. But your friend, Lieutenant Schmidt has indicated to the press that you are less than bright. Your fugitive status seems to upset him."

"Me too."

"I don't know about that," drawled Fred. "Seems to me it's gotten you food, valet service and my bed."

"I appreciate your help."

"Don't embarrass me. You'll get a bill."

We laughed.

"I do have more news for you."

"Which is...?"

"I telephoned a few poor souls who might be worried about you, your lady love, Elizabeth, and your suffering confessor, the good Father Daniel Brendan Fahey. Elizabeth wants to nurse your wounds and Father Fahey offers you his professional services. I assured them that you are as all right as you ever are."

"Thanks. You called the only people I would have."

As well he should, for Fred, Elizabeth and Father Dan had all known each other for years, all felt genuine affection for the other. The only difficulty was between Fred and Father Dan. Father Fahey, in his official capacity, disapproved of Fred's lapses from virtue, although he sympathized with Fred's tragic double-bind, being a gay who loved his Church. On this subject they were implacable foes and Fred was not above baiting the Padre.

"When you spoke to Elizabeth did she mention Kathy Adams?"

"I spoke with Miss Adams. She was so relieved, and I believed her the seventh time she said so."

"She's a good kid."

"I guess so." He shook his head. "Are you assembling a harem when not killing people? Performing unspeakable acts on nubile little things?"

"Of course, I am. I dangle her from a rafter, flog her and commit unnatural deeds upon her body. It sure beats watching television."

"There's hope for you."

Between more rounds of banter I ate breakfast and telephoned Elizabeth and Kathy. I told them to do nothing until I came to see them this evening. As far as I was concerned, I said, our plan for meeting the Mertons was still on. Only after taking care of the meeting, win or lose, would I turn myself in to the police. A few days delay could not get me in any more trouble. Killing Bad Trip Leo had made it impossible for me to disappear as planned, and that was the only regret I felt on Bad Trip's account.

I also phoned Father Dan to tell him that I wanted to come by to see him. He told me that that was fine by him, provided I didn't burst into his rectory with blazing six shooters. My friends were trying to convince me I was a cross between John Wayne and Dirty Harry. Some friends.

Fred and I played chess all afternoon while listening to seventeenth-century opera by Cavalli—like two retirees killing yet another day. It was unreal, but it allowed me to relax, to gather strength. My sense of well-being remained through our early evening dinner of spaghetti with a garlicky clam sauce. It was nearly seven o'clock and the evening fog had already darkened the sky.

"I'm going to Father Dan's now," I said.

"Me too," Fred announced.

"You don't have to go with me."

"I want to. Besides, I wouldn't want to miss any of your gunfights on the way."

"Funny."

"It's for your own good. An extra set of eyes and ears couldn't hurt." He was very serious. "I also have the advantage of vast experience in knowing how to ride the Municipal Railway to the Church."

"I'm sold."

When Fred and I began our walk down to Market Street I was filled with apprehension. Being on a street brought the memory of my shootout and flight too vividly to mind. I began to sweat despite the fog-chilled evening breeze, a weakness in my legs made them seem to not be mine. Every person we passed on the street had a hint of menace to him. It was an indiscriminate paranoia that applied to well-dressed businessmen, street corner winos, little boys racing from store window to store window, bag ladies on their endless wandering, and the tired-looking hookers making their way toward Union Square. If I bore the mark of Cain, they all wore the number of the Beast.

The ride on the streetcar was no better. As the half-filled streetcar swayed its way along the tracks I became convinced that my fellow passengers were all Harry Salomon's hired assassins. When the streetcar entered the long Market-Castro tunnel I felt the suffocation of premature entombment. It was not a ride through a tunnel; it was a descent into Hell in a car full of demons. And, believe me, my fellow passengers could have come from central casting for a zombie movie. There were the zitty punks with faces showing bored, cruel stupidity; there was a young girl junkie, emaciated and muttering to herself; even the solid citizen types had a look of barely restrained desperate hatred for this lot. When the streetcar emerged into the foggy night at the end of the tunnel I was near panic. Fred was a good companion. Aware of my dread he tried to divert my mind with his witty, erudite talk. Relief brightened his expression when the streetcar finally arrived at our stop.

Father Fahey opened the door of the rectory. "What have you done to Farnigan!" he exclaimed to Fred. "He looks worse than Lazarus called from the grave."

"He was fine 'til we came here."

"Bob wasn't acting sickly before?"

"Not at all. We had a pleasant afternoon. His mood was excellent considering his caper as a one man crime wave."

"Much too much has happened to the man."

I interrupted, sick of being odd man out.

"Could you two finish the autopsy inside? I'm scared silly and standing under a porch light isn't doing me a fucking bit of good."

They shut up and hurtled me into the rectory's living room. I got the chair that did not face the horrific painting of the Crucifixion, a gruesome, blood drenched rendering. The painter would have loved Charley Cudder's human demolitions.

"Bob, I'm going to give you a drink." Father Dan looked unsure. "You have a tendency to be a souse, but from the way you look, this snort is purely medicinal."

"Thanks."

"Scotch. Lots of it. Just a little water to take the edge off."

"Words of a drinking man."

He looked at Fred. "I can find some wine for you, I think."

"Or turn some water into wine if need be."

"Don't mock miracles, Fred. You'll probably end up needing some yourself."

While we had our drinks I explained to Father Dan the events that had taken place since I last visited him and my plans for tonight. When I had finished he was beyond controlling his rage. The big priest jumped up from his chair and stormed about the room like a demented offensive lineman.

"I told you," he roared. "I told you that such people were a pit of iniquity. They mock God, abuse the innocent, and destroy. Thanatos is death, and their gangster friends are death's agents. I always said these cults—damn them—are tools of Satan and now you tell me they are also tools or allies with the criminals." He shook his head. "What's going on? Is the whole world mad?"

"Always has been," Fred offered as a comment.

I said, "Where there is any money you find the Harry Salomons trying to work their way in. Though there has to be more than just the extortion angle, some link to Salomon's other interests. Thanatos is probably caught up in something bigger than Doctor Stone's mumbo-jumbo con."

"Don't tell me there's no Original Sin." Father Dan fumed as he sat back down. He looked at me and asked, "Are you up to following your plan?"

"I think so—much as I don't want to. It's something I have to do, though."

"Good."

"With that vote of confidence, I think I'll phone Elizabeth and tell her I'm on my way."

I went out to the hallway where the private rectory phone was and dialed Elizabeth's number. No answer. I redialed with the same result. After all that had happened maybe I had gotten confused. Looking down at her number in the phone book between each digit I dialed, I tried again. No answer. A profound sickness filled me.

"There's no answer." I gasped as I entered the living room. "Something is very wrong."

Father Dan was decisive. "We'll take my car." He looked at me. "You have your gun?"

"In my pocket."

"Let's go."

Father Dan's car was parked outside in the church parking lot. It was a five-year-old Buick sedan, an eight-cylinder pollution special. I sat in the front seat next to Father Dan, Fred was in the back. We pulled out of the lot and began the fastest ride I had taken since my car was new. Father Daniel Brendan Fahey may do a good job obeying God's Law, but his sins against the motor vehicle code were legion that night. After a near miss with a stalled moving van, three barely avoided intersection collisions, and terrifying countless pedestrians, I knew why Holy Wars are the worst of all.

I was almost thrown through the windshield when screaming brakes announced our arrival at Elizabeth's. We rushed to the front door. It was unlocked. I glanced at my friends, took my gun from my coat pocket and stepped inside and ran up the stairs.

There was no warmth or order or comfort in the house now. Rage and a sense of desecration filled me as I looked at the destruction. Shattered pictures, broken lamps, overturned chairs, and other wreckage, the pathetic ruins of a life's belongings, lay before me. No Elizabeth. No Kathy.

Anger and bewilderment filled the faces of Fred and Father Dan.

"Look in the other rooms," I said.

Fred headed toward the kitchen, Father Dan followed me to Elizabeth's bedroom. Empty. We proceeded to the guest room. There, on the bed, lay Elizabeth. Alive.

Father Dan yelled, "The bastards!"

She lay on the bed, her legs and arms tied, her mouth stuffed with a pillow case. Elizabeth's face was bruised and puffy, one darkened eye already had swollen closed. It looked like her nose had been broken. Dried blood, black and caked, covered most of her face. Terror had flashed in her eyes when we entered, flickering anew when Fred rushed in from the kitchen. As I removed the gag she began to sob.

Father Dan was untying the rope that bound her legs, Fred was fumbling with the rope that tied her arms. I was holding her head, whispering to her that all was fine now.

Turning to Fred I said, "See if you can find something for her to drink."

"Right."

He left.

Elizabeth was sitting up in bed as I sat next to her holding her hands. Father Dan had brought a damp wash cloth from the bathroom and was gently wiping the blood from Elizabeth's face. Leaning over her from the other side of the bed he said, "No one will hurt you now." To me he said, "We should call a doctor."

Elizabeth shook her head. "Not now. I don't want a lot of questions." She began crying again. "Poor Kathy. They have her."

"Take this Elizabeth," said Fred who had come in with a teacup. "There's some brandy in it. Drink it. It'll help." Her hands shook as she held the cup to her lips. She winced with pain as she drank—the brandy burned the teeth cuts in her mouth from the beating.

Elizabeth repeated, "They have her."

"Who?"

"I think it was the men who hurt you, Bob. A thin man and a big one."

"Hal and Charley."

"Yes. I heard the thin one call the big one Charley. Charley hit me." She began moving restlessly. "I want to sit in a chair, Bob."

Fred and I helped her to a small chair near the dresser. Fred returned to the bed and sat on it next to Father Dan while I knelt next to Elizabeth's chair and held her hand. She sat straight and rigid, eyes fixed on somewhere far away; her hand had a sickly, cold dampness as it lay in mine.

"Tell us what happened," I said.

She stared silently.

"Please try."

Father Dan moved to the other side of the chair. "Elizabeth, I know you're hurt and that you want to be alone with yourself," he said. "But we can't do anything unless you tell us what you know. Remember, Kathy's in great danger now. Talk to us."

"They took her."

"When?" coaxed Father Dan.

"After dinner."

I asked, "What time?"

"Seven-thirty." She looked at me, life returning to her face and eyes. "Boris Farnigan, you, of all people, know that dinner is at seven."

"Silly me."

She laughed and we hugged each other gracelessly as I half rose and she bent over. "Silly you," she said.

With no more prompting she told us of Kathy's abduction.

"It was a little after seven-thirty," she began. "I had left the dinner dishes in the sink and Kathy and I were watching television in the living room when the bell rang. Like a thoughtless fool I went downstairs to answer it." She gasped. "It's my fault, isn't it?"

"No, no." I said. "Hal and Charley get in wherever they want. They have shitty manners."

"Don't swear, Bob. But thank you." She looked thoughtful. She found my explanation plausible and continued. "Anyhow, I went and opened the door. The big one—Charley—grabbed me, pinned me against the wall with a hand over my mouth. He said he would kill me if I made any noise. Hal—the little guy—was holding a gun. Hal said that Charley would let me go and I was to walk upstairs slowly, saying nothing. I did. Charley went first. I followed him with Hal behind me with the gun." She stopped and looked at Fred. "Fred, would you get me some more brandy?"

"I live to serve, Elizabeth."

After she had drunk some more brandy I asked her, "What happened upstairs?"

"I guess Kathy thought that something was odd. When Hal, Charley and I had almost reached the top, there she was at the head of the stairs. I suppose she had gotten curious. Kathy saw Charley and turned and ran to the living room. Charley chased right after her. I would have run, too, but Hal jammed the gun in my back. There were bangs and crashes from the living room."

Elizabeth shuddered. She looked at all of us, in turn, very slowly, very intently.

"Go on," said Father Dan. "We're here."

"When Hal and I got in the living room Charley was holding Kathy. She was kicking at him. Kathy had one free hand and was scratching at Charley. He hit her. Three...maybe four times ... and she fell." Her eyes filled with tears again. "She lay there moaning. I think she was more out than awake. She wasn't dead. Then," she added.

"She'll be all right," I said. In my heart I had a sick ache.

"You really think so?"

"Yes," I lied. "I'll find her and she will be fine."

"I hope so. Those men are animals. They hurt her."

"Tell me what happened to you, Elizabeth."

She took a deep breath. "I panicked. I tried to run to Kathy. She looked so helpless and so hurt there on the floor that I didn't care about Hal and his gun—she needed me."

Just like Elizabeth not to care about herself when anyone else was suffering, I thought. She continued. "But Charley shoved me away. He called me a bitch and a slut. I ran out of the room. Charley was behind me and I couldn't shut the door"— her eyes moved in the direction of the guest room door—"before he was there. He punched me. I've never been hurt like that before. I fell and the room started to move."

"I'll kill him," I said.

To my surprise she nodded and said, "He is evil and deserves to die."

I glanced at Father Dan, daring him with my eyes to babble any "Judge not lest ye be judged" bullshit. He was in no mood to preach, I guess, because all he did was squeeze Elizabeth's shoulder with his hand a little harder for a second.

Fred said, "If Bob doesn't kill him, I will."

We were all shocked. All of us knew Fred's horror of violence, despite his wickedly cutting way of talk.

"I believe you would," said Father Dan with lingering disbelief. "And I'd forgive you—or Bob," he added.

I spoke up. "Let Elizabeth finish her story." We all looked at her and she resumed.

"Charley lifted me from the floor. I was helpless, ready to

black out. He threw me on the bed and tied my arms. Then he stuffed that pillow case—part of it—in my mouth. That woke me up, brought me back to life. I was squirming, kicking now." She blushed. "I kicked him between the legs—you know what I mean—while he was trying to tie my legs. That's when he started hitting me again. I think he wanted to kill me."

"He probably did," I said.

"I was almost unconscious when he stopped. That Hal person had come in and was yelling to stop, that he wasn't supposed to kill me. He told Charley to finish tying me and then come help him carry Kathy to the car. Hal told Charley to remember that they had two more people to get."

"The Mertons," I said.

"Who?"

"Kathy's Aunt and Uncle."

Elizabeth's eyes widened as new horror filled her. "Oh no! They're going to kill them all!" She stood up suddenly, but Father Dan and I grabbed her, making her resume sitting.

"Time for more brandy," said Fred as he left the room. He returned with the bottle in a few moments.

Elizabeth sobbed with a deep, hopeless abandon, the kind of crying that leaves one shaking inside. Father Dan and I were both holding her. Finally, she stopped crying, accepted the new cup of brandy from Fred, and leaned back in her chair. I resumed my position, kneeling and holding her hand.

"So then they left?" I asked.

"Not before Charley hit me one more time. He knocked me out."

And he probably broke the living room for a little extra fun, I thought.

I kissed her. Never had I felt so inadequate, so hopelessly unable to help. I loved this woman and had only brought her pain. Elizabeth had suffered for loving me for many years, and now I had allowed the sickness of the criminal streets to invade her life, to destroy, and to inflict pain. This was my fault. You must realize by now that super-gumshoe Farnigan had allowed himself to be followed the day he had driven Kathy to Elizabeth's. I vowed to burn my detective license when this was over —if I survived, and if the cops didn't take it from me first.

The room was silent except for occasional mumbling from Elizabeth. Her breathing was getting slower and heavier, her body sagged in the chair, and sleepiness was stealing over her face.

"Do you want to lie down?" I asked.

"In my own bed. Not in here."

We all assisted her to bed in her own room. She was both exhausted and a little drunk. To my surprise she fell asleep as soon as we lay her blanket over her, clothes and all. We left the room to go to the living room.

"She can't be left alone," I said.

Father Dan answered. "I'll phone St. Monica's Hospital. I know I can rouse Sister Brigid—she's a nurse—and have her come. If Elizabeth needs treatment Sister Brigid will get it for her. Otherwise she'll be a good companion."

"Phone," I said. As he phoned, I turned to Fred. "I have to go after Hal and Charley. It's almost midnight right now and they have a hell of a head start."

"I'm coming with you."

"So am I," said Father Dan as he waited for an answer to his call.

Before I could reply Father Dan began speaking to St. Monica's Hospital. Fred and I stood silently and listened to Father Dan make contact with Sister Brigid. When his conversation ended, he said, "She'll be here in ten minutes."

"Then I have ten minutes to tell both of you that you can't come with me," I said shaking my head to ward off any reply.

"I've already fucked things up. Hal and Charley hurt Elizabeth and snatched Kathy because I let them follow me. People get hurt because of me. I'm not risking my two best friends." I stuck my hand out towards Father Dan. "If you will give me your car keys I'll be on my way. I've lost lots of time."

"You'll get the keys if you can take them from me," the beefy priest said. He sounded like he meant it.

Fred spat out his words. "Listen, big shot, Elizabeth is my friend, too. After what I've seen you'll leave without me only if you fight me."

It was too much for me, both of them were yelling at me. Not too loud, though. Even in their anger they did not want to waken Elizabeth, frighten her again. I cleared some rubble from the sofa, sat, and raised my hands.

"I give up. If you two get killed, don't blame me."

"I certainly will," Fred said indignantly.

The tension broke with our dry laughter.

"We'll go to Thanatos," I said.

"What about the Merton's place?" asked Fred.

"It's not likely anyone's there, but we can stop. It is on the way."

Father Dan held out the car keys, "I guess you want to drive."

"No, you drive. At least to the Merton's. It's easy to get to. Thanatos is a little trickier, so I'll drive there."

"Fine."

"We should call the cops," I told them. "But I'm afraid they'll eat up too much time with idiot bullshit questions. No offense, you two, but I think our worst will be quicker than their best."

We spoke very little after that as we waited for Sister Brigid. She was late and full of excuses. The good Reverend Father took her in to see Elizabeth and explained a little of the situation. Sister Brigid did not approve and insisted on having a resident physician come over from the hospital. We said that was fine—but no cops. Her scruples were being tested almost beyond endurance. Like so many nuns do, she was looking at us with the stern eyes of one who believes all men are merely aging delinquent boys, but when she said that she would follow our instructions we believed her. Believe me, you had to. This was a big, tough, very formidable nun—like all the ones who have terrified countless generations of school kids, and have been loved, too.

It was twelve-thirty when we finally drove off under the watchful eye of Sister Brigid who stood in Elizabeth's doorway. No doubt she was glad to be rid of us.

‹

CHAPTER 26

What more can I say about Father Daniel Brendan Fahey, Scourge of the Roadway? Believe me, our ride was more of same: a high-speed succession of barely averted accidents, complete with blaring horns and shrieking breaks. I can't count how many times the dirty digit, that eloquent middle finger, was flipped at us. The only good deed that we may have done was, perhaps, to have frightened a few of the late night drunk drivers into a sudden, chilling sobriety.

Father Dan had gone down to 25th Avenue, through Golden Gate Park, and from there driven onto the Golden Gate Bridge from the Presidio. The bridge was covered with fog, the sharp, damp chill matched my cold heart. Each of us was silent, our thoughts best kept to ourselves. I was again tormented with the insistent vision of me, Farnigan, as guest of honor at his own wake, compliments of Thanatos and Harry Salomon.

My reverie was broken as we rode down the Waldo Grade on Highway 101, the bridge a few miles behind us.

"Highway Patrol," said Father Dan.

Sure enough, a blaze of red and white lights from the patrol car danced in the night. "End of the line," I said. Fugitive Farnigan caught in routine traffic stop, the headlines would say.

"Shut up," the Reverend Father snapped. "I'll get us through."

Visions of a high-speed chase brought a tremor of excitement and nausea over me. But no, it was not to be. Father Dan was pulling over to the shoulder of the highway.

"Not to worry," he said. "I'm going to use my Roman collar for all it's worth. Just pray the cop's no Catholic hater."

The patrol car had stopped behind us on the shoulder, the flashing lights a source of comfort to the other drivers now passing by—grateful our misfortune was not theirs. I watched the patrolman approach the driver's window.

"Going a little fast tonight," he said, giving the perennial opening line. "May I see your license?"

The cop was young, maybe in his late twenties, one of those tall, muscular types with impassively boring good looks. He was coldly eying each of us in turn. So far he had not shone his flashlight into the car. I was hidden in darkness, a silhouette. He was inspecting Fr. Dan's driver's license.

"You were doing seventy, Father," he said, ready to lecture.

"I know, I know," replied Father Dan, his voice soft and rueful. "I was in the wrong. I offer no excuse, but I was in a terrible hurry."

That interested the cop.

"An emergency, Father?"

"Yes. A poor soul in Fairfax. I fear that he may have brought harm to himself. My self and his two friends here fear that he may have despaired."

"You're saying he might kill himself, Father?"

"There's no telling what can happen to a man when his folly comes home to him." Father Dan shook his head in sorrow. "We went to offer him comfort and perhaps save him from destruction."

(My God, what a man, I thought. He's describing Uncle Skip for sure but leading the cop to draw his own conclusions. I should have known that Father Dan would find a crafty way to juggle the truth without offending his scruples with a lie. Even in my state of dread I admired Father Daniel Brendan Fahey's skill.)

"Be that as it may, Father, seventy miles an hour is too fast." He pondered the crime. "But I'm just going to warn you. I want you to observe the posted speed limits the rest of the way to Fairfax. Understand?"

"Of course, Officer. I can't thank you enough. God bless you."

"Thanks, Father." The cop added, "I'm not a Catholic but I respect you priests."

"I'm grateful to you. You'll be in my prayers."

The cop gave Father Dan his license, enjoined us to practice safe driving, and wished us luck in Fairfax. Father Dan filled the air with thanks, blessings and promises of good driving. The man could lay it on without shame.

Back on the freeway we drove in silence, still nervous, as the patrol car followed behind us. Father Dan drove no faster than fifty miles per hour until the cop got bored and turned off in Corte Madera. Fred spoke first.

"You'll get some time in Purgatory for that performance," he said with good humored malice.

"No lectures from you, Fred Morton. You do not have the subtlety of mind for the fine convolutions of moral theology."

I sat in silence as they argued minuscule distinctions, priest and medievalist rising to new heights of windy debate. Their words floated over me as I brooded over my narrow escape, my growing fear for the Mertons and Kathy. We had exited the freeway to drive out Sir Francis Drake Boulevard, and it was only as we approached Fairfax that I broke my silence to give directions for getting to the Mertons' home. Father Dan acknowledged this only with a furious nod, resentful of my intrusion on the great debate.

"This it?" asked Father Dan as he stopped the car in front of the Mertons' sorry duplex. I nodded.

The front door was unlocked. Gun in hand I entered first. It was dark inside. After a few moments of agitated fumbling I located the light switch and flicked it on. I was looking at the third torn up home I had seen in as many days. I guess even Uncle Skip had had enough manliness left in him to fight against this invasion of his home. The thought of what Charley Cudder must have done to Uncle Skip's thin, shaky body gave me a feeling of sick weariness yet again. It was Fred who pointed to the blood on the floor. There was a lot of it soaked into the beige carpeting.

"Someone's probably dead," I said.

"Both of them, I'm afraid," said Father Dan coming into the living room. "While you two were gaping at the mess in here, I looked in the bedroom back there. Blood's all over the bed, the floor, even the wall. It looks like a butcher shop."

"I guess they both fought," I said.

"They both lost," murmured Fred.

I went into the bedroom. It was something out of a gory movie, the type I closed my eyes in. Someone, probably good old Uncle Skip, had been a human pinball, flung from wall to bed to floor and back again, Charley Cudder battering him into human garbage. Charley Cudder, pinball flipper. I did not want to believe what I saw and tried to see some hope where there could be none.

I returned to the living room and spoke.

"It looks bad back there. I'm sure that it was Merton himself that got it in there, but..." I paused with an air of significance. "There are no bodies. It's just possible that the Merton's left here alive."

Father Dan shook his head. "One of them, at best, left dying after the beating in the bedroom."

"They're both dead," said Fred, heavy conviction in his voice. "This is a death trip."

"We can't be sure," I insisted. "Okay, maybe old man Merton is dead—should be by the looks of things—but maybe not. The old lady probably didn't get that god-awful of a beating. She could be alive. We don't know. So let's assume that the old lady is still breathing. And maybe Merton, Uncle Skip, is as well."

My friends looked dubious. Believe me, I couldn't blame them. But this was time for hope—any hope—no matter how fragile, and how wishful. I babbled on.

"I figure Hal and Charley are taking the Mertons and Kathy to Thanatos."

Father Dan held out his car keys. "Shut up and drive, Bob. We have to save whoever we can."

CHAPTER 27

The Fairfax-Bolinas Road is no fun in the daytime. As I have said, it is narrow and snaky. At night it's plunged into near total darkness. Tonight was particularly bad, for the fog had moved inland from the coast, not too thick but dense enough to obscure vision. I had to drive more slowly than necessary to avoid missing the side road to Thanatos. Getting lost would be cruel luck even for me. It seemed I had driven at least eight-hundred miles before the headlights illuminated the shabby sign that marked the road to Thanatos New Age Meditation and Cremation Society. I swung the big Buick onto the dirt road, stopped, and turned the headlights off.

"I don't want to announce our arrival," I said. "There's enough light to make out the road with just the parking lights on. It's a straight road through the trees to where the ashram and crematorium are, not far at all. We can't stray from the road because of the trees." I paused and saw my friends nod. "The parking lot—such as it is—comes at the top of a small rise. I'll stop near it, and we'll go the rest of the way on foot."

Again, they nodded. I was relieved that Father Dan didn't object. He should understand that I would be using his Buick to block the road. Maybe he hadn't thought that out. Believe me, I wasn't going to offer any enlightenment. He and Fred could argue about my failings in moral theology later. Father Dan said, "You know the way."

Fred added, "Drive on, Sherlock."

I turned on the parking lights and began the slow ride up the hill. The big car inched forward at a little less than five miles per hour, and I could feel the engine straining to surge forward. It was a rare experience to have so much power available to me from a car. Believe me, sometimes my Impala's top speed was what I was doing now. I wondered if I would ever drive my old, much abused car again. For that matter, would any of us ever drive again?

Before I could get too self-piteous the parking lot loomed before me. I turned the parking lights off immediately, cut the ignition, and let the Buick coast a few feet at an angle before braking it to a halt.

It was quiet, too silent for endurance. We got out of the car, taking care to make no noise, and stood together facing the ashram fifty feet in front of us. No cars were in the lot, though perhaps there would be room to hide one in the rear of the ashram, or at the rear entrance to the crematorium beyond. A bare light bulb was lit over the doorway to the ashram; the crematorium was similarly illuminated. Although both Father Dan and Fred were obviously tense and edgy, like me, they were fascinated by the sheer ugliness of the ashram. I could tell. In the dim light the amateurish paintings of the Hindu deities on the wall had a cheaply sinister look. Each had an aspect of menace.

"This is an evil place," whispered Father Dan. "It mocks the spirit."

Fred agreed. "It's sick, Farnigan."

"Tell me about it."

"Ugly, too. One look at this and you would want to die."

"We're talking too much," I said. "I say we go inside the ashram. See what's in there—if anything."

Since the windows of the former ranch house had been boarded over for the so-called art, I saw no reason not to walk directly to the door. Once we were at the door I figured that Father Dan and Fred should stand one at each side while I entered. Remember, I'm the boy with the gun. They nodded agreement to the plan and we set out across the parking lot.

For once things worked out as planned. Gun in hand I was standing inside the candlelit ashram. There was the over-whelming sharply sweet smell of sandalwood scented incense, and there was another stronger odor. I smelled gasoline. Fred and Father Dan entered.

"Empty?" asked Fred.

"Think so. There are other rooms, though."

"Too quiet."

"I'm sure it's empty, Fred."

"No, it's not," said Father Dan as he pointed toward a tapestry which covered a side door, the way to Dr. Edmund Potter Stone's office. Emerging was a man carrying a gasoline can. It was Ralph, the devotee of Thanatos I had talked to on my first visit. He was moving as if unaware of our presence.

"Stop," I shouted. "I have a gun."

That got Ralph's attention. He leaned back against the wall, a bewildered look on his face. The gasoline can dropped to the floor. Father Dan and Ralph moved across the room to stand one on each side of Ralph. I was standing a few feet in front of Ralph.

"I'm hurt," he said.

"He is, Bob," said Fred. "Look at his shirt. Its bloody."

Ralph seemed to remember me. "Our Guide's friend shot me," he said. "Why me?"

"I don't know."

"They tried to kill me." He laughed. "but they didn't. If my old lady can't kill me—God knows she tries—they can't kill me."

"May I look at your wound?" asked Father Dan.

Ralph nodded and gingerly lifted his bloodstained blue work shirt. Even I could tell in the poor light that it was only a superficial wound, the shot had barely grazed his lower left rib cage. More blood than damage and the bleeding had already stopped. Nonetheless, Father Dan hovered around as if he knew something about medicine. Priests love to be experts.

Father Dan announced, "He'll live." To Ralph he said, "You should see a doctor."

Ralph, lowering his shirt, said, "I'll hitchhike to town in the morning."

Father Dan shrugged his shoulders.

"You the only person here?" I asked Ralph.

"Just me." He shook his head. "Thought I was dead, they did. They all left."

"Who?"

"Doctor Stone, his assistant in the crematorium—that's Calvin—and the two men, a big one and a short guy."

My voice trembled. "You didn't see a girl—a young woman?"

"Sure did. They kept her tied up in the car. The same car poor Mr. and Mrs. Merton came in. Big guy got Mr. Merton out of the trunk."

"Dead?"

"I don't know about the rest of you, but if I looked like he did, I know I'd be dead."

"Mrs. Merton? She dead?"

"Not then, I guess. Could have been. Carried her into the crematorium. The big guy did. Just like with her husband."

Father Dan and Fred started moving toward the door. They stopped when Ralph continued speaking.

"Don't bother," said Ralph. "They went up in smoke." Ralph looked placid, but I could see the horror on the faces of Fred and Father Dan. All but Ralph made the sign of the cross. I could see Father Dan's lips moving in prayer. Uncle Skip and Aunt Juliet were now a few charred bones and smoke in the night fog. And one of them may have been alive when entering the furnace.

Bitter, I broke the silence. "They finally got something for all their money."

Ralph chortled, a sickly little rattle without meaning. Fred looked stunned.

"Farnigan, you go too far," Father Dan said with disgust.

"I'm sorry, but it's true. Thanatos took everything from them —their money, their health, their free will, and at the end their lives. Their pre-paid cremation is all they ever got for it. The Mertons were suckers who paid more than most other losers. Believe me, it has a ghastly humor. The literal last word in con jobs."

Fred walked out as I spoke, not wanting to hear anymore. That, and the look on Father Dan's face as he listened to me, made me hate my own cynicism, for part of me grieved with an ache I had not known in years. Perhaps he could see that too, the me behind the words.

"You're not as bad as you talk," he said.

"I hope you're right."

I turned to Ralph who appeared lost in his own thoughts. "You're not part of all this are you, Ralph?"

"Me? No. Part of nothing, anymore. I don't know about the rest of you, but I'm having no part of this place. Not after I saw what I saw."

"The Mertons."

"Enough for me. The Guide is not a good man." He scratched his head. "Maybe the old lady was right. I should've kept my money. We fought about it again tonight. That old bitch can make my life hell. She raised so much hell I hitch-hiked out here to be by myself, maybe see the Guide."

"What time was that?"

"Nine-thirty, maybe ten. Should have stayed home. I always could have hit the old lady." He looked sorrowful. "No, I gave that up when I stopped drinking. Another mistake."

"It's no mistake, Ralph," said Father Dan.

Ralph's eyes narrowed. "You a priest?"

"Yes, I am."

"You wouldn't know about it then."

Father Dan chuckled in spite of himself.

I asked, "The men with the Mertons and the girl were already here?"

"No, they came later. When I got here only the Guide, Doctor Stone, and Calvin were here. Goddamn Guide told me to go home." Ralph was indignant. "Said I had no business out here at night. He said that after all the money I gave him. Hell, I even helped paint some of the fancy pictures out front."

"But you didn't go," I coaxed.

"No. I walked around in the trees behind the crematorium trying to calm down. I didn't want to mess up my fucking karma. Must have been out there for an hour or so before everybody else arrived." He began to whisper. "I watched them. I saw it all —like I told you."

"But they saw you, too."

"Damn it all, they did. I don't know about the rest of you, but when I sneeze it wakes up the cows in the next county. Goddamn sneeze almost took my damn head off. The little shit hears it, draws a gun, and comes running into the trees. I ran like a son of a bitch. He shoots at me, two or three times. He's a lousy shot. Misses me. I keep running and he's right behind, maybe twenty-thirty yards."

"He did shoot you, though."

"Hell, yes. The little bastard got lucky. He blasted me and I went flying down the goddamn hill to the dry creek bed. Smug little fart figured he had killed me. Didn't even climb down to see if I was dead."

"You're lucky he didn't come after you," I said. "The little fart is a professional killer."

"Damn right."

"What happened then?"

"I don't know about the rest of you, but when I'm shot, I lay still until I'm sure I'm not bleeding to death. That's what I did. For about twenty minutes. Then I decided to get the hell out of there. My side hurt like hell when I climbed out of the gulley.

"Anyhow, I worked my way back to the bushes by the crematorium. I watched them go. They all left together. The big guy and the little guy with the gun went in their car, actually, a pickup truck. They followed Doctor Stone and Calvin."

I almost begged Ralph, "Do you have any idea where they were going?"

"Sure. To the landing."

"What landing?"

"The one about ten miles north of Point Reyes." He looked at me as if I should have known. "That's where they keep the boat they use to take the ashes from the crematorium out to sea. I'm sure that's where they were going. I heard them talk about going to the landing earlier."

I had one last question. "Was the young woman still with them?"

"Think so. I thought I saw somebody in the back seat of the car."

"We have to go there," said Father Dan. He turned to

Ralph. "Do you know how to get there? To the landing?" Ralph did and gave us detailed directions.

Father Dan and I started toward the front door to leave when I turned around to see Ralph holding the can of gasoline again. I asked the obvious question, "What's with the gasoline?"

"I don't know about the rest of you, but when they fuck around with me I get even. Soon as you all leave this whole place is going up in smoke—like the Mertons."

"You're a good man, Ralph," I said.

"Be careful. And God bless you," added Father Dan.

Ralph said, "Yeah, yeah."

We left.

CHAPTER 28

F red was waiting outside in the cold. He glared at me. As we walked to the Buick Father Dan began explaining (a) where we had to go next, and (b) why I really was not the bastard I seemed to be. Fred looked dubious about both propositions.

When we reached the Buick, I got into the driver's seat.

Since Father Dan had not asked for the keys, I assumed the chauffeur job was mine for keeps. The padre sat next to me, Fred in back. Father Dan was still explaining my hidden virtues when I started the car. I turned the Buick around in the parking lot and drove back down the dirt road to the Bolinas-Fairfax Road where I turned right. It was going to be a treacherous ride on this windy, rutted road until it intersected with Highway 1 where we would go north toward Point Reyes. Only the thought of Kathy Adams made me press on. Add to that something I knew about Harry Salmon and young women.

Father Dan and Fred had fallen silent. Each of us was lost once again in our own worries, fears, grievances and faint hopes. We had gone for about five miles in tense quiet when, as the

Buick rounded a curve at the top of a hill, Fred yelled for me to stop. I did, turning around in my seat to look at him, as did Father Dan.

"Look," said Fred as he pointed out the rear window. A dull red glow filled the foggy night sky in the distance. "Ralph did it," Father Dan said. "Burned it like he promised."

"Thank God for arson," I murmured.

The priest had heard me. "Thank Him for acts of purification."

"Either one," I said as I began to drive again.

The priest and Fred decided to discuss eschatology, gleefully pondering the many obscure prophecies about the end of the world, the final conflict, and the promised Judgment. Naturally, they rambled on and on concerning prophecies of fire, both men inspired by Ralph's conflagration at Thanatos. This stuff is all very interesting in its way, but I could not stop myself from thinking about other judgments and their meaning. What about the Mertons' fiery end, the hot lead that tore into Bad Trip Leo's chest, and all the inflamed passions, griefs, and tears of all of us involved in this late hour race with death? To be sure, God will destroy the world (and good riddance), but I weary of all the little Armageddons played out on mean streets, dirty alleys, and hate-filled homes. I felt myself ready to fall into a frenzy of self-pity and wished that someone would tell a dirty joke. Or start singing "Ninety-nine Bottles of Beer on the Wall."

About two miles from the intersecting of the Fairfax-Bolinas Road and the Coast Highway a fire engine's lights glowed in the fog and ocean mist as it approached us. It stopped the end of the world jabber.

"Ralph sets a good fire," I said approvingly.

"The fire must have spread to the woods," said Fred. "I hope they don't find Ralph. Thanatos did enough to him without his having to take an arson rap."

Father Dan shook his head. "I'm afraid Ralph is the sort of man who stays around to watch his handiwork and tell everyone about it."

"I don't know about the rest of you," mimicked Fred, "but when I get mad I torch places."

We all laughed.

I wondered if the firemen would have laughed too. Poor Ralph.

I made the turn north onto the Coast Highway. In many ways this stretch of Highway 1 is called a highway only as a courtesy; the narrow, twisting, two-lane road that winds its way along the coast is dark and lonely. Only a few small towns, coming far apart, break the monotony of driving on it. In daylight, if it isn't blotted out by fog or mist, the gray ocean views have a somber beauty, and the high wooded hills beyond a narrow stretch of flatland to the east offer dappled relief. At night, Highway 1 possesses no virtues, except little traffic. Tonight we passed few other vehicles and made good time in the Buick. So good, in fact, that the town of Point Reyes Station came as a surprise.

Despite Point Reyes Station's attempt to hide Highway 1 within its limits, I drove through with minimum confusion and continued the lonely drive into the night. Father Dan and I discussed Ralph's instructions for getting to the boat landing Thanatos used. For Ralph, the instructions were remarkably lucid—we hoped that was no illusion. As described, the property would not be hard to spot. We should find a dirt road marked by a sign informing the curious passerby that it was a road privately owned by Thanatos and to keep off. We planned to ignore that warning. The road would run about four hundred feet until coming to a gate, part of a high chain-link fence topped with barbed wire.

"What's a fence doing there?" asked Fred. "Did Ralph explain it?"

"Normal security, I guess," said Father Dan, then he added thoughtfully, "but it's dimensions bother me."

"Apparently the fence runs for about three hundred yards," I explained. "At each end it turns and goes about another five hundred or so yards down to the ocean, in fact, it runs a little way out into the water."

Fred commented, "A lot of fence."

"Over rough country, too. Ralph told me and Father Dan after going through the gate everything slopes down sharply. Lots of rock, heavy brush and deep ravines from the winter rain run off."

"The road gets pretty nasty, according to Ralph, narrow, bumpy, and bordered by gulleys," added Father Dan.

"The landing dock and boathouse are at the end of the road by a little stretch of sand," I said. "It's not going to be easy getting in, getting Kathy, and getting out."

"Has anything involving you ever been a breeze?" asked Fred.

"No, and it's not likely to change."

"Business as usual for you, Farnigan."

I only nodded and looked down at the odometer. If Ralph was right, we were within a mile or two of the landing. I told Father Dan and Ralph to start looking for the dirt road and the sign.

As we looked for the road in silence, my thoughts reverted to the only thing I didn't want to think about, Harry Salomon and Kathy Adams. It had long been a dirty secret known to those of us who walk the uglier streets: Harry Salomon was a sadist, his sexuality cruel. For years there had been stories of young prostitutes nearly beaten to death by Harry in his elaborate acting out of dominance fantasies. A pimp I know, Rupert Armand, once told me as we drank in an after-hours Tenderloin bar of a young hooker that Harry Salomon had killed. Harry, it seems, had a taste for sex and strangulation; he gained his satisfaction from choking his partners again and again, tantalizing himself by playing a god of life and death. Lucky girls survived the ordeal; the unlucky one had died. Armand heard that not only had Salomon felt no remorse, but was thrilled when the battered hooker died in his hands. After that, Harry was said to have developed a taste for death, and the trouble with Harry is that he usually got what he wanted.

As best as I could make out the only reason Kathy was alive, if she was, had something to do with Harry's perversion. It figured, I thought, that Harry Salomon would want to combine business and pleasure, to avenge himself for Kathy's interference by killing her in a special way.

I told them of my fears.

"There's a special torment in hell for his kind," Father Dan said. "All my training tells me not to assume any man's damnation, not even that of Judas Iscariot; but a monster such as Harry Salomon surely is among the eternally lost. The bastard."

The priest's voice was low and bitter with implacable condemnation. A Medieval image of the book slammed shut and the altar candles extinguished to the tolling of bells filled me with nervous awe.

"Anathema sit," I muttered the ancient words of excommunication.

"Yes," said Father Dan solemnly. "Let him be damned."

"There it is!" yelled Fred. "The sign!"

Ahead on the left, barely visible in the fog and mist, was the unfriendly sign warning of Thanatos' private road.

"Goddammit," I said as I swung the car onto the dirt road.

The Buick's rear end had tried to skid, the tires had let out a shriek.

"Shit," I said, "I don't want them to hear us."

"Don't worry," said Fred. "I suspect we're a good distance from the landing."

"I can't screw this up. I can't let this one fall apart. I have to save Kathy."

"Quiet," said Father Dan. "The gate's ahead."

Through the gloom I could see the high fence and gate. I eased the car to a stop, and we got out to inspect the gate. It was a standard affair, secured by a chain and a padlock.

Fred asked me, "Can you open it?"

"Probably. In normal times I have to pick a lot of locks." I had my very illegal leather bound case of lock picking tools in hand. "If I can't do it like a pro, then a tire iron can break the chain. Maybe."

I set to work on the lock. It was stubborn and the fact that my hands were shaking and cold didn't help. The headlights didn't provide the best light. Fred and Father Dan hovered around, feet shifting nervously.

"Back off," I told them. "I can't see with your shadows getting in the way."

They retreated a few steps and I was back to my fumbling. "I've got it," I said as I felt the lock give. The padlock was now in my hand; Fred came forward and pulled the chain off.

"Not bad," said Fred.

I grinned. "I'm a professional, you know."

"Let's swing the gate open," said Father Dan impatiently.

A few moments later we were on our way. As Ralph had promised the road was rutted and surrounded by high brush and scrawny trees. I had the parking lights on as the Buick crept forward; we were lost in fog and mist and shadow. I noted that the winter rain's runoff had cut deep trenches along the side of the road.

"Where's the landing?" breathed Fred.

"I can't see a thing."

Father Dan whispered, "We have to go downhill a way according to Ralph."

As the car edged forward, I became aware that we were beginning to slope downward toward the ocean, but the foliage wasn't thinning out. This was a stretch of coastline where brush grew down almost to the water's edge, no lush, sandy beachfront here. From the gate the road curved to the right, no doubt to avoid the deeper gulleys and ravines that marked the way to the sea. Now the road was beginning to straighten out again, and the angle of descent grew sharper.

"We're close," I whispered. My companions said nothing. "I should stop soon."

"Then what?" asked Fred.

"I don't know," I snarled. "I can't think of everything."

"Some fucking professional," sneered Fred.

I was furious, but Father Dan spoke up before I could. "Quiet, you two. The important thing is that we're here."

Fred snorted.

Desperate, I said, "I'll stop the car, then we sneak up on them. The big thing is to get Kathy. If we get that done then we try to make it back to the car."

"Look!" yelled Father Dan.

The road had run out. Before us, maybe thirty yards away, was the ocean. I saw the pickup truck from Thanatos, Hal and Charley's sedan, and Harry Salomon's Mercedes parked in front of the brightly lit boathouse and dock. It was a tight fit for all those cars in the narrow clearing. The boat, a twenty-foot cabin cruiser, was moored. On the dock stood Hal, Charley, Harry Salomon and Salomon's chauffeur. They were watching Dr.

Stone and his flunky, Calvin, lift a heavy box, about the size of a large trunk from the boat. I did not see Kathy.

"End of the line," I said as I stopped the car, turned off the engine and switched off the parking lights.

Luck had run out; we had been spotted. Hal and Charley were running toward us, guns in hand.

"Out," I yelled. "Jump into the brush."

I swung my door open. My feet almost slipped on the dirt and gravel as I hurled myself into the gulley at the side of the road. I could hear Father Dan and Fred making the same desperate scramble. I also heard the sound of three shots from the guns of Hal and Charley.

I raced into the thick brush, clawing my way through the tangle of branches that tore my clothes and scratched my hands and face. About twenty feet into the brush I stopped, panting and disoriented. My eyes had adjusted to the dark and I could make out shapes vaguely. There was noise to my left, the sound of men fighting their way through the dense growth. I reached into my pocket and grabbed my gun. Motionless, I waited as the sounds of men came closer. At last sound merged into a shape, one that I recognized. Five yards away from me was Father Dan.

"Over here," I said in a stage whisper.

I had to repeat myself, louder, before he responded. "I see you," he said. "Fred is behind me."

In less than a minute my friends were standing next to me.

"You both okay?" I asked.

There were nods.

"Either of you see Hal or Charley?"

"I think they're still up by the Buick," said Father Dan.

"Probably," I said. "I hear no noise, so I guess they're not searching the brush for us yet."

"Unless they're listening to us right now," said Fred. "No. If they heard us, they would be shooting."

Father Dan asked, "What now, Bob?"

I thought for a moment before I whispered, "Hal and Charley will be coming after us. I suspect that Salomon will send his chauffeur—his name's Bill, I think—into the brush near the landing."

"They could just leave," Fred objected.

"No, they can't. First of all, our car blocks the road—and I have the keys. Second, they can't let us run free."

I saw Fred nod.

"I'm assuming," I continued, "that they will hunt for us figuring that we won't be coming for them." Father Dan and Fred both nodded. "Like I say, Hal and Charley will come for us up here, Bill and maybe Calvin will be moving in from below us. We only have one gun, my gun, so I'll have to take care of Hal and Charley."

"What about us?" asked Father Dan.

"You and Fred work your way down toward the ocean. Arm yourselves with rocks or sticks or whatever, but be quiet. Position yourselves down there and wait for me. In this light if you're quiet and stay in one place I don't think it'll be easy for them to find you."

"I don't like it," Fred muttered.

Father Dan hissed at him. "Got a better idea?"

"No."

"Then it's settled. We do as Bob says."

"You two had better start moving," I said. "Good luck."

Fred stammered, "You're taking too much risk, Bob."

"Forget it. Remember, I've got the gun." I smiled at both of them.

When they had begun making their way through the brush, my thoughts turned to the problem at hand. Should I go for Hal and Charley or wait for them to come to me? I stood for a few moments in motionless indecision, my great mind not at work, when the question was answered for me. Hal and Charley came into the brush looking for us.

I now knew why they had delayed their pursuit—I could see the glow from their flashlights cutting through the low fog that shrouded the brush. One of them, probably Charley, must have gone back to the boathouse for them, granting us a short reprieve. The flashlights made it easier for them, but it had the same effect for me. Sure, they could spot me easier, but I also had illuminated targets. Part of me was insulted. Hal and Charley were underestimating me; they felt that no advantage they gave me would be of any use. The flashlights were a sign of their contempt for me. Hope told me that Hal and Charley would pay for their arrogance; experience made me doubtful.

About thirty yards separated the glow between the two flashlights. Hal and Charley were not very far into the heavy growth yet. I decided to head in the direction of the light furthest from me. Again, progress was slow and loud as I struggled to keep my balance on the uneven terrain while grappling with the branches that assaulted me. I had not gone far when I realized that Hal and Charley had switched off their flashlights. It was to be cat and mouse in the dark after all. While their action restored my belief in their intelligence and soothed my ego, it struck me that my life was devoid of any and all breaks. Farnigan's Law of Universal Perversity was recalled without welcome: The opposite will always manifest itself in direct contradiction to the expected or hoped for.

As quietly as possible, I continued in the direction of where I had last seen the light farthest from me. My body was aching with tension as I tried to see some sign of movement, some shape that would disclose itself as that of a man. I had gone about a dozen more yards when I decided to stop, to listen for sounds of movement other than my own. I was aware of blood running down my cheek from a scratch a thorny branch had lashed across my face.

I heard no sound from my left, but to the right someone was very close. My eyes were stinging and watery from the strain of trying to see my stalker through the gloom, but I could not see my hunter who sounded closer every second. I decided to crouch down so that I could not be seen.

As I lowered myself into a crouch, my fat butt brushed against a brush and a branch snapped loudly. Shots immediately burst through the darkness ten feet to my right. I fired four times in the direction the shots came from and rushed forward from my crouch. Without thought or fear I raged through the dense whipping branches and vine laden undergrowth. I was determined to confront my enemy face to face.

The world turned upside down as I tripped over a heavy object. I lay sprawled out and winded on the ground, the pungent smell of wet earth and broken leaves was overwhelming. As I scrambled to my feet, I saw that I had stumbled over Hal. He lay on his back and when I touched his belly, I bent over and felt the warm stickiness of blood. Charley Cudder had lost his only friend forever, I thought, as I wiped my bloodied hand on Hal Smith's jacket.

Before I had a chance to think of my next step, I heard Charley. Fear swept over me as the night filled with the sound of Charley bursting his way through the brush and undergrowth. He was howling Hal's name over and over again. Charley's voice was hoarse with rage and desperation. I grabbed the flashlight near Hal's outstretched left arm and, kneeling, pointed it in the direction of Charley Cudder's charge. I switched the flashlight on.

The sudden light must have blinded Charley. He was twenty feet from me, moving like an irresistible force, his face red and distorted from exertion and anger. I could tell that as he ran into the light, he was unable to see me. Charley yelled, "You bastard, Farnigan!"

I squeezed off a shot.

The bullet slammed into Charley Cudder's gut but he neither stopped nor fell as he lurched on ahead. But he had dropped his gun and flashlight.

I fired again and the bullet, thanks to my shaking hand, merely grazed his side.

He roared, "I'll kill you!"

Charley was only a few feet away when I pulled the trigger again. I heard the dull click of an empty gun as Charley ran full force into me as I began to stand.

Charley Cudder covered me. I could smell his sweat, blood and rage. The force of the collision with Charley had left me dazed as I lay with the breath largely knocked out of me. He had a knee shoved deep into my stomach as one hand closed around my throat while the other hard and crushing, punched me above the left ear.

"You bastard Farnigan," he yelled again. "I'll kill you, fucker!

With my right hand I tried to break his grasp on my throat as I desperately groped with my left hand for my flashlight. His fist had cocked to hit me again when I felt the cold metal of the flashlight. Using what strength I had I squirmed and stretched under Charley's weight with the flashlight in my hand. I swung it with all the force I could muster. It made a sickening sound when it landed above Charley's right temple. He moaned, and the grip on my throat released as he toppled over. Before he could move I was on top of him as he had been on me.

The bullet wounds and the blow to the head had sapped the strength from Charley Cudder's body. He lay helpless as I battered his head with the flashlight.

When I stood up finally, the flashlight was a hollow, dented shell with no batteries inside, they had flown into the bushes along with the top of the flashlight.

Charley Cudder was as dead as the flashlight.

I had killed another man, someone whom I wanted to kill because he caused me pain, fear and humiliation, but I had no thrill, no bloodlust satisfaction. All I could think of were my endangered friends and Kathy Adams.

Staggering about, weak, breathless and exhausted, I found the two dead men's guns and Charley's intact flashlight. I put the extra guns in my pocket to give to Father Dan and Fred. Then I reloaded my gun.

It seemed to me that I was probably alone in this part of the Thanatos enclosure and that it would make it fairly safe to use the flashlight for a while as I moved toward the ocean front and my friends. To my surprise, the light didn't really make my going any easier, all it did was let me see that the dense growth was as hard to penetrate as it seemed. Maybe that was why Charley Cudder had run through the darkness without using his light. Then again, Charley may have been too goddamn stupid to think of his flashlight. For sure I couldn't ask the late, dumb bastard. It felt good to think ill of the dead.

Everything vanished from my mind when I heard the gunshots from the distance. Someone was shooting at Father Dan and Fred. I switched off the flashlight and threw it to one side as I began to run, such as I could. Better to run in darkness than to be a lit target—rest in peace, Charley.

As I pushed my way through the endless branches and bushes, I heard no other shots. I did hear shouting from where I thought the landing was. What I mainly did was mindlessly fight the foliage, no longer really noticing pain or exhaustion.

It was as if my body no longer cared. Yet I had some awareness, for it became evident that I was very near the ocean. The smell of the sea and sound of surf registered first. Then I noticed that the brush was getting less dense, but that the fog and the ocean mist were thickening. My footing was even more treacherous as I came upon shallow, dry channels that had been cut by the run off of winter's rains. I had to slow down. The slowing down robbed me of momentum and I soon stood still. My heart was threatening to smash through my rib cage, my breathing alternated between wheeze and death rattle. I felt dizzy and the universe was getting darker.

CHAPTER 29

I had blacked out. Too out of shape, my body had called a halt and forced me to rest. I must have been noisy about it, too. Noisy enough to summon help from Father Dan who heard the fall of Farnigan.

As I came to, Father Dan was whispering, "Are you all right?"

"Yes...I think so."

"Fred and I heard the shots from up there."

"I killed Hal and Charley."

"My God," gasped the priest. After a silence he added, "I'll pray for them later."

"What about you and Fred? I heard shots too."

"Fred's been shot, Bob."

My eyes filled with helpless tears.

"He's not dead, is he?" I asked.

"Thank God, no," said Father Dan. "We made too much noise and Salomon's man—Bill, you called him—started shooting. I don't think he even saw us—he just shot wild. But he wounded Fred."

I sat up. "Take me to him."

"You think you can walk?"

"Yeah. My head's clear enough."

Father Dan helped me to my feet. I was unsteady at first, but as I followed Father Dan some unexpected reserve of energy came to my aid.

"Don't worry about the punk," Father Dan said. "They called him back to the landing."

"When?"

"Almost immediately after he shot at us. A matter of minutes."

I pondered for a moment before saying, "I guess Salomon had figured out by then that Hal and Charley weren't coming back. He wanted his boy by his side."

"Sounds good." The priest laughed without humor. "I'll take any break we get."

Father Dan had scarcely finished speaking when I saw Fred. He was lying on the ground, unconscious, with a bloodied piece of torn shirt wrapped around his head as a bandage. I knelt down and grabbed Fred's left arm to feel for a pulse. It was there, strong and steady.

"Not as bad as it looks," said Father Dan. He put his hand on my shoulder. "The bullet got hair and skin only."

Standing up I said, "We have to get him out of here to a doctor."

Father Dan nodded and reminded me that we couldn't do anything until we took care of Salomon and friends. There was also the matter of Kathy Adams. We were stuck here.

"I haven't heard any movement from them," said the priest.

"We have to do something before sunrise," I said. "Dawn is probably just an hour or so away and we'll sitting ducks in the daylight." I reached into my pocket and held out a gun. "This was Hal or Charley's. Can you—will you—use it?"

He nodded as he took the gun from me and said grimly, "I'll do what I have to. It's my duty to Fred and that poor girl."

I took off my coat and covered Fred, having first shoved my gun and the extra gun between my belt and ample gut.

"Let's work our way over to the edge of the clearing by the landing. Once there, we check out Salomon and his men, and make our plans."

We made our way through the brush to the edge of the clearing in about five minutes. From behind a heavy clump of bushes we had a clear view of the well-lit landing as we knelt together in silence. Salomon, the chauffeur, Dr. Stone and Calvin were standing together behind Salomon's Mercedes. They were using the car as a wall between them and us. Behind the standing men was the pickup truck, car and truck having formed a makeshift enclosure about as wide as another car. No sign of Kathy Adams. I had no idea what to do now. Salomon and his chauffeur, Bill, were both armed, and it was likely that Dr. Stone and Calvin had guns too. So a frontal assault seemed out of the question. I could sense Father Dan's desire for me to tell him a brilliant plan. All I could do was not look at him. I stared at the men behind the Mercedes and thought.

Then we heard voices. An argument had broken out. I could not understand the words over the drone of the surf nearby. But Salomon and Bill were yelling at Calvin. Calvin had a scared, panicky look, was waving his arms about, giving all the signs of a man who knew he was in too deep. The chauffeur, bodyguard, really, stepped forward raising his arm menacingly at Calvin. Dr. Stone was cowering next to Salomon.

We did hear Calvin yell, "You can't stop me!" Panic had overcome caution as Calvin pushed the surprised Bill aside and ran-past Stone and Salomon. He was heading up the dirt road. Calvin wanted out of it all and Bill obliged him. Calvin took three shots in the back from the bodyguard's gun.

"Mother of God," whispered Father Dan.

Bill walked up to Calvin's sprawled body and kicked it off to the side of the road into the ditch. I was tempted to take advantage of this chance to have a clear shot at the bodyguard, but I failed to see what would be accomplished other than giving our position away. I needed a plan before I did anything.

As I watched, Bill returned to the Mercedes. Salomon looked at Dr. Edmund Potter Stone and then nodded to Bill. Both Bill and Stone understood Salomon. Harry Salomon was cutting his losses. Now.

Stone made for the dock. Maybe he thought he could find safety on the boat or walk on water. Stone knew that Calvin had gotten nowhere but dead on the road. As Stone ran down the dock, Bill stood at the rear, slowly and deliberately raising his .38. The bodyguard squeezed off two shots. The force of impact kept Stone hurtling forward in a crazy stagger until he ran out of dock and fell into the ocean. Bill had a look of professional satisfaction as he walked back to Salomon.

"They're devouring their own," said Father Dan.

I looked at him and said, "We'll be next."

"There's only two of them, and they don't seem to want to come after us."

"Don't get optimistic, Dan. I've had a very pessimistic thought."

"What?"

"You know what Salomon is?" I asked and answered myself. "He's an executive. A captain of industry, criminal division."

"So?"

"Like all the other executives he's got all the best. All the modern up-to-date gadgets. I expect he's got a radio on the boat."

Father Dan groaned. "Shit, hell and damnation."

"You got it. Help's on the way. That's why Salomon and Bill

can sit around and do nothing. Somebody's corning to clean up the mess."

"You're saying it's all over, Bob." His tone was weary and sad.

"Unless my idea works." I paused. "Is your car insurance paid up?"

"What has that to ...? Yes, of course it is."

"Your Buick's going to be worse for wear, Father."

My brainstorm would depend on Salomon's cavalry taking a little more time to arrive. If they showed up soon all bets were off and Elizabeth Casey would have a lot of dead to mourn. The plan was heartbreakingly simple. I would work my way to the Buick which I figured could take no more than ten minutes even traveling through the brush. To be safe, Father Dan would time me for twelve minutes and then open fire to create a diversion while I got into the car and started it. I would push the accelerator to the floor and race the Buick downhill, brake fast and hard, running it between the Mercedes and pickup. This would get Salomon and his bodyguard into the open where Father Dan would have a clear shot at them. I, of course, assumed that I would survive the destruction derby in good enough shape to help.

Even in the dim light, I could read the skepticism in Father Dan's face. If I had any doubts his words and tone of voice cleared up that lack of understanding.

"Better than no plan," he muttered and added, "At least, I guess so."

"Got anything better?"

"No."

I handed the priest my extra gun. "Take this. You'll need all the firepower you can get. For God's sake don't use up all the bullets before I hit the car and truck." I hesitated. "You do know how to shoot a gun?"

"Yes."

"Learn that in the seminary too?"

"A parishioner bought me a gun and taught me to shoot it. He said the church was in too rough a neighborhood for me to be unprotected. A gun can scare off a lot of trouble." He snorted. "I never had trouble though—until you showed up."

"Bitch about that later," I said. "I'm going now. Start timing me."

"Good luck, Bob."

"Pray for me. It's your job."

"Move along. I'll handle the prayer and shoot straight."

CHAPTER 30

I began the ascent to the Buick.

I made better time than I had predicted and arrived near the driver's side of the Buick without hearing anything from below. There was also, thank God, no indication of any more of Salomon's men having arrived at the top of the road. So I waited for Father Dan to begin shooting, having edged up as close to the car as I could without exposing myself. It seemed as if I waited long enough to have read War and Peace. Fear began to send ripples of giddy nausea through me as I began to worry about Father Dan. But surely, I reassured myself, I would have heard something if he had gotten in trouble. So I waited and waited until desperation began to fill my mind. As it turned out, the good padre was dubious about my stamina and general physical condition: he gave me extra time. I wish I had known that then. My state of mind was such that when I did hear the gunfire from below it took me a moment of dull stupidity to recognize what it was.

I sprang for the car and hurled the door open, throwing myself forward flat on the seat. Bending my body more than I thought possible, I put the key in the ignition as my foot found the gas pedal. The Buick roared to life. I huddled behind the steering wheel trying to give as small a target as possible.

The shatterproof windshield began to shatter when the first bullets hit. I pushed the accelerator to the floor and the powerful V-8 engine gave the car a surging thrust forward. I don't think I really had the car under control as it shot down the hill.

In front of me I saw the parked Mercedes and pickup truck coming ever closer. Salomon had run to the side of the boathouse away from Father Dan. Bill was standing between the car and pickup shooting. The Buick was swaying and skidding as I fought for control, never taking my foot from the gas pedal. The windshield had gone now and my face was covered with cuts from the flying glass.

The Buick squeezed between the Mercedes and the pickup. Metal against metal shrieked as sparks flew from the sides of the Buick. Bill, his face frozen with surprised horror, had not followed Salomon to safety. His body disappeared under the car. The Buick crashed through the boathouse wall and stopped when the engine died with a jolting shudder.

I had to lay on my back on the glass covered seat to kick the dented door open. When I emerged from the ruined Buick, I crouched at its side and looked out the torn hole in the boathouse wall. Outside I could hear Father Dan calling me, telling me to come out.

I ran outside. Father Dan was standing by the trunk of the Mercedes. I looked at the car and the pickup. The Buick had driven a powerful wedge between them and had moved each several feet. I did not see the bodyguard's body on the ground. Father Dan read my mind.

"He's underneath the Buick."

I shuddered. "That's what killed the engine."

The priest looked ill.

"Where's Salomon?"

"Anywhere, Bob." The priest pointed. "The last I saw him he was ducking around the side of the boathouse. I guess he's in the brush."

I had an idea. "You wait here," I said as I began running down the dock to the moored boat, certain that Salomon was working his way around the boathouse and through the water to the boat.

When I stepped onto the deck of the cabin cruiser, I heard a splashing sound from forward near the prow. I ran along the deck toward the sound and saw Harry Salomon, wet and frightened, on his hands and knees. He had just pulled himself aboard. Salomon's eyes filled with fear and hatred when he saw me and my gun.

He started to say something as, rising, he reached for the gun in his shoulder holster. I shot before he said a word. It was a clean shot to the chest. The impact hurled Harry Salomon back into the sea to join Dr. Edmund Potter Stone in death.

I felt the boat rock as Father Dan jumped aboard. "I'm all right," I yelled. "I killed Salomon."

"They're all dead, then," he said as he came up to me. "They deserved no better."

"It was them or us," the priest muttered, "but, still ..."

I interrupted. "We have to find Kathy. She still may be alive."

We got off the boat and ran down the dock to Hal and Charley's car. Kathy wasn't inside.

"The trunk," suggested Father Dan.

"No. Ralph said she was in the back seat." I shivered. "If she's been moved, it was to the Mercedes for Harry's pleasure."

"Do you think he ..."

"Don't say that!" I ran to the Mercedes.

Kathy Adams was not in the backseat of the Mercedes. But,

lucky for once, the keys were in the ignition. I had not relished the thought of prying Bill loose from the underside of the Buick to search for the keys.

"Hurry, Farnigan," pleaded Father Dan as I fumbled with the key to the trunk.

The trunk door sprang open. Kathy Adams lay in front of the small footlocker we had seen being taken from the boat earlier by Calvin and Dr. Stone.

"She's breathing," I said. "Barely."

We lifted her from the trunk and placed her on the ground. She had not been harmed as far as I could see. There were only the livid bruise marks on her upper cheek and forehead from her struggle when kidnapped. I massaged her wrists while Father Dan dabbed her forehead with a handkerchief he had moistened in the ocean. After a few minutes she began to stir.

"She's coming around, Bob."

"Thank God." My will pleaded with her to regain consciousness. "I couldn't stand to lose her."

Her eyelids fluttered and then opened. For a moment she didn't recognize us and fear filled her eyes. Then, just as quickly, she smiled.

"I knew you would come, Bob," she said in a faint voice.

"I've never lost a client. Been fired often enough—but I've never lost one."

"You always joke with me."

"Not always."

She tried to sit up. "What about Elizabeth?"

I held her and said, "Elizabeth is fine." I paused. "Your Aunt and Uncle are dead."

"I know," she whispered and began to cry.

She cried on my shoulder for about a minute before Father Dan spoke.

"We should get out of here," he said. "We still have to get Fred, too."

I looked up at Father Dan and nodded. "We'll put Kathy in Hal and Charley's car and then go get Fred. I'll find a way to start the car and we'll leave."

I explained to Kathy that Fred had been wounded and that Hal and Charley's car was our only undamaged means of transportation. "I know you don't want to be in that car again, but it's all we can do."

"I understand."

Father Dan and I got Kathy in the car and set off to find Fred. There was a hint of dawn breaking as we entered the brush yet again. Fred was semiconscious and dithering. We got him up on his rubbery legs and walked him to the car. Kathy, though weak and possibly in shock, decided to baby Fred.

I said to Father Dan. "I have to know what's in that footlocker in the Mercedes."

He nodded.

I snapped the lock off of the footlocker with the Mercedes' tire iron and opened it. The locker was filled with plastic bags containing a white powder. I opened one.

"It's cocaine," I announced.

Father Dan said, "So that was their nasty trade."

I began to explain what an ideal cover Thanatos had been, how the boat must have taken the crematorium's ashes out to sea and brought back cocaine. I guessed that the cabin cruiser from Thanatos either met another larger boat or that maybe a buoy with the coke inside was at a prearranged spot for the cruiser to pick up. I was beginning to expound at length when we heard the sirens. A Marin County Sheriff's car was coming down the hill.

I said to Father Dan, "I guess Ralph didn't get away."

He nodded. "Poor bastard."

CHAPTER 31

So that was that.

The Marin County Sheriff, soon to be followed by contingents from the California Highway Patrol and even representatives of the San Francisco Police Department, arrived after Dan, Fred and I had done all the work. Believe me, I would have thought that they would have been grateful. But, no, they were models of resentment, a reaction to the paper work we had caused. The deputy who accompanied me as I led him to the dead grew more agitated as we stumbled about the brush in the gray dawn.

"Jesus," he said as I showed him the remains of Hal and Charley, "did you have to kill them all?"

"Kill or be killed, you know."

"I guess."

"Look at it this way. Better than a bunch of unsolved killings."

The deputy shook his head. "Maybe."

"More work for you guys if they had nailed us."

"No," he said.

"Why the hell not?"

"From what you say they would have killed you and taken your bodies back to the crematorium for disposal."

"So?"

"No corpses. No murders to be solved." He smiled in triumph. "Just three or four missing San Francisco residents for the City cops to worry about."

"You don't expect an apology?" I asked.

He thought that over. At last he said, "Just promise to stay in the City in the future."

This sort of sympathy abounded throughout the day and on into early evening. Kathy and Fred had been taken to Marin General Hospital and Father Dan and I were being questioned at the Marin Civic Center, a complex designed by Frank Lloyd Wright on one of his off days. Everyone was getting into the act. The FBI and the Coast Guard had also sent quiz masters to question Dan and me separately and together. Father Dan was released before I was. He was not anxious to leave as he said his goodbyes.

"I have to face the Archbishop," he said. "I think I'd rather be here with you."

"Yeah, cops don't bully priests."

"I don't know about that, Bob. They've been none too friendly." He shook his head. "The Archbishop will be furious."

"I thought he was big on activism in the Church."

"Only in Latin America." With a sigh he added, "If only Harry Salomon had been a Salvadorian landowner ...."

"An accident of geography."

"The accident was knowing you, Bob."

"Thanks."

"I have no regrets. We did the right thing," he said hastily.

"Even if you end up in a home for wayward priests."

A deputy came into the room where we were talking and politely informed Father Dan that it was time for him to go, which he did. The deputy yelled at me. More questions to be answered.

Yelling at Boris Farnigan became a national pastime. Even after the cops finally let me go late that night I had a week's worth of loud voices to bear. District Attorneys in two counties shouted, but they pressed no charges. Lt. Schmidt shrieked about my irresponsibility, but did not lift my investigator's license. Irma the landlady was still hysterical about my alleged liberties with her body, but she was not going to evict me (against her better judgment, she claimed).

The truly good news was that my friends were all okay—and still friends. Kathy, Elizabeth, and Fred were out of the hospital, Father Dan was not defrocked, and the D.A. in Marin decided not to prosecute Ralph for arson. Not bad.

Unbelievably, the newspapers, after a few dark mutterings about vigilantism, decided that I, Boris Farnigan, was a hero.

I would have been proud if I could believe it.

To celebrate all of this good fortune, I invited all of the living principals in the Thanatos Affair to my apartment for a party, a substitute for the wake I had foreseen. Within my limited budget I spared no expense. I ordered cold cuts and other goodies from a real delicatessen, bought good liquor, and even attempted to make my apartment look habitable. Believe me, it is not easy to be a host when your home belongs in a set for a Depression film.

On the day of the party I started drinking wine about two hours before the guests arrived. I was in a blissful stupor as I sat on the sofa watching my company, hearing only occasional snatches of conversation. They all seemed to enjoy each other and I could tell as the conversations grew louder that they did have enough to drink. Now and again, someone would try to engage me in party talk, but I only wanted to communicate with my wine glass. Although I deeply cared for each person present, to one degree or another, I wanted only to watch them, to enjoy the sight of them being alive after so much death. So I sat and observed, content in my heart and in my wine.

The only time I rose from the sofa was when Estelle Brinton phoned. I guess it was because Salomon and I had made the papers, but it tied up everything. There was a sad and wistful undercurrent in her elegant voice as she once again thanked me for trying to save Melissa. I could offer her only the thought that Harry Salomon had paid his dues. We both knew that could never stop the forever pain. I drank more deeply and quietly when I returned to the sofa.

I guess that the party lasted about three hours before it was time for everyone to go home. One by one each guest came into my hazy view to say goodbye. I can remember each person's leave-taking because of the mixture of affection and regret in their words.

Irma was drunker than I was.

"Good night, Farnigan."

"'Night, Irma."

She twisted her face in an approximation of a smile.

"I'm glad they didn't kill you. At least you usually pay your rent on time." Irma continued, more to herself than to me. "Maybe I should have rented this flat to that nice Chinese couple. I bet they didn't know any goddamn gangsters."

Irma muttered her way to the door.

"I've got early Mass to say, Bob," said Father Dan. "I have to go."

"The Archbishop isn't threatening you about your job, is he?"

"His Excellency gave me one hell of a lecture, you know; but in the end he only cautioned me to be more careful in the friends I choose to have." He laughed. "I could have told him that."

And so Father Dan exited.

I didn't remember inviting Lt. Schmidt to the party, and so I was surprised when he came to say goodbye. He told me that it was all right after all that I had survived, but he wished he had run me in that night at the American Hotel.

Ralph replaced Lt. Schmidt in my blurred vision. "The old lady told me not to come tonight," Ralph announced.

"I'm glad you did."

"Hell to pay at home."

"Sorry."

"I don't know about the rest of you, but it's good Thanatos is out of business; I should have burnt it down a long time ago. The old lady says it was the only smart thing I did."

Ralph wandered off. I wondered if he regretted not torching his old lady.

Next came Fred, wearing the bandage on his head like a crown of martyrdom.

"The next time you're playing desperado, forget where I live," he said.

"And deny you the chance for adventure?"

"My life is quite exciting enough. If I live to die of boredom at a ripe old age, that's as rugged a life as I desire."

"You have a point, Fred."

"We'll talk about it over dinner. Food, wine and music is all we need, Bob."

"I'll be there."

"Leave your gun home."

I was alone for a few moments before Elizabeth sat down next to me. The bruises on her face had lightened and were mostly hidden by her makeup. Her voice was low and intense with emotion.

"We almost lost each other," she said. "I feel responsible."

"You're responsible?" I asked. "How? You did all you could. You don't think you should have been able to stop Hal and Charley?"

She clasped my arm. "Not that, Bob. I was thinking that I could have made our lives different."

"They are what they are, Elizabeth."

"I suppose. But we can change them—together."

"Maybe we will."

"Do you mean that?" Her eyes searched my face.

"Yes."

"Come and talk to me."

"I will," I said. "When I haven't been drinking."

"That would be best."

Maybe I should move out of state, I thought, and felt immediately guilty. Sympathy for Ralph's marital woes filled me.

"I'm going now, Bob."

"Goodbye. I'll call tomorrow."

"I'll be waiting."

Elizabeth left.

Now only Kathy Adams remained. She sat across from me on one of my kitchen chairs that had found its way to the living room.

"Not an easy night," she said as she lit a cigarette.

I nodded. "The people who care about you complicate everything."

"Is it worth it?"

"We all have regrets, but I really wouldn't change things. Somehow there's something right about it."

"That's what I've been telling myself these last few days." Her voice began to tremble. "I have to believe that it was right of me to interfere in Uncle Skip and Aunt Juliet's lives."

"It was, Kathy."

"They're dead."

"I don't think there was any way to save them. From the time they hooked up with Doctor Stone they were on their way to death. My only regret is that it was so horrible."

"Regret is a weak word," she said in a distant tone of voice.

"It's the only one I can think of. Regret is on my mind. You, Elizabeth, Dan—all of you—have regrets, and so do I. That's what has been on all of our minds tonight. We lived through a tragedy, Kathy. It's only normal that we have doubts and regrets."

She murmured, "We did the best we could with what we had."

"To be sure."

"I don't regret knowing you, Bob," she said after a long silence. "You're special to me. Don't ever think I regret that we made love."

"I wouldn't do that."

We talked some more. The wine had made both of us willing to talk about the things in our lives that had gone wrong, but there was no self-pity. Regret was part of the process of living, we concluded.

Finally,
all
regrets
noted,
I
grinned
and
nodded,
suddenly
weary.
And
Kathy
exited.

The End

Printed in Great Britain
by Amazon

53253129R00130